FROSTBITE HOTEL

KARIN ADAMS

James Lorimer & Company Ltd., Publishers
Toronto

Copyright © 2014 by Karin Adams
First published in the United States in 2015.

James Lorimer & Company Ltd., Publishers acknowledges the support
of the Ontario Arts Council. We acknowledge the financial support
of the Government of Canada through the Canada Book Fund for
our publishing activities. We acknowledge the support of the Canada
Council for the Arts which last year invested $24.3 million in writing
and publishing throughout Canada. We acknowledge the Government
of Ontario through the Ontario Media Development Corporation's
Ontario Book Initiative. We acknowledge the financial assistance
provided by the Manitoba Arts Council.

Cover Design: Megan Fildes

Library and Archives Canada Cataloguing in Publication

Adams, Karin, author
        Frostbite Hotel / Karin Adams.

Issued in print and electronic formats.
ISBN 978-1-4594-0706-0 (pbk.).--ISBN 978-1-4594-0707-7 (bound).
--ISBN 978-1-4594-0708-4 (epub)

        I. Title.

PS8601.D453F76 2014   jC813'.6   C2014-903032-0
C2014-903033-9

James Lorimer & Company Ltd., Publishers
317 Adelaide Street West,
Suite 1002
Toronto, ON, Canada
M5V 1P9
www.lorimer.ca

Distributed in the
United States by:
Orca Book Publishers
P.O. Box 468
Custer, WA USA
98240-0468

Printed and bound in Canada.
Manufactured by Friesens Corporation in Altona, Manitoba, Canada in
August 2014.
Job #205571

For Nathan and Storm

#1
"Identify a Problem"

"We need a *problem*," said Kirby Katz to his best friend Marvin DaSilva.

Outside the second-storey window it was a pitch-black, blustery, middle-of-winter Sunday night. The wind shrieked and howled. Snow swirled and eddied under the streetlights' beams. Kirby and Marvin were snug, holed up as usual in Kirby's tidy bedroom playing video games. Only Kirby wasn't playing. He was sitting in his 'thinking chair' beside his bedroom window, reading his brand new book about business. It was called *How to Make Something from Nothing* by William T.

Williamson, billionaire hotel tycoon.

"What are you talking about?" Marvin asked, his eyes zoned in on the screen. He sat on the floor, frantically jabbing at the triggers and buttons on the controller in his hands.

"'*Identify a Problem*'," Kirby read, tracing his finger over the title of Chapter One. Most Grade 5 kids idolized hockey players or singers or actors on TV. For Kirby, who had dreamed of becoming a successful businessman since he was six, there was no bigger hero than William T. Williamson. He'd made a million dollars by the time he was fifteen. *Fifteen!* That was only four years away for Kirby. That's why Kirby made sure to read all of William T. Williamson's books, including *From Windows to Riches* and *They Said I Was Nuts!*. Kirby was sure the latest book *How to Make Something from Nothing* held the last key to success. If only he could "identify a problem" just like William T. Williamson advised . . .

"Ugh!" Marvin groaned

in disgust and tossed his controller aside. On screen, he'd just been squished by a toppled tower of blocks.

Kirby barely noticed as Marvin restarted the game. He didn't hear the winter wind rattling his house like the hollow bones of a skeleton. Kirby was too busy churning the words he was reading over and over in his brain. In fact, he wasn't aware of anything but the book in his hands.

"*When people have a PROBLEM,*" Kirby read out loud to Marvin. "*It means that something is missing in their lives. What's missing is the SOLUTION and that SOLUTION is your BUSINESS. That's why it's very important to start your business by identifying a PROBLEM.*"

"I don't get it," Marvin mumbled. He angled his controller desperately in the air as he manoeuvred through another set of hazards.

Kirby put down his book and rose from his chair. He felt his brows crease as he sank deep in thought. William T. Williamson had started out washing windows with a pocket full of loose change. By fifteen, he had his own window washing company. A few years later, he opened his first 'Golden W' Hotel. Today, according to his autobiography, *The Man Behind the W*, William T. Williamson owned a whole *chain* of 'Golden Ws', ran seven international charities, wore 100% silk ties every day, and spent his holidays parasailing in the Pacific Ocean. This guy knew what he was talking about!

Kirby began to pace the floor. "A *problem*, Marvin!" he said. "Like our dog-wash business last summer. Hot, dirty dogs — that was a *problem*."

"Yeah," grumbled Marvin. "The dogs kept knocking over our buckets and drenching us. That was a problem!"

Kirby paused and sighed. Marvin was right. 'Not-So-Hot-Dogs' had created more problems than it had solved. "Okay — what about the time we decorated people's driveways with sidewalk chalk art?" said Kirby, resuming his pacing. "Boring driveways — another *problem*."

"How much money did we make on that?" Marvin asked. "Like, a loonie in total? Ah, *nuts*!" he groaned as he was suddenly smothered by a pile of digital bricks. Marvin snapped off the game and leaped to his feet.

Kirby couldn't argue with his friend. None of their business ventures had been particularly successful. At least not the way Kirby imagined they needed to be if he was ever going to walk in the footsteps of William T. Williamson. That's why it was so important to get it right this time.

"Whoa," Marvin said, looking out the window. "It's like a major blizzard out there!" Marvin leaned toward the frosty pane of glass for a better view. "You can barely see my house. Wonder if they'll cancel school tomorrow?"

"Hmm," Kirby said, still lost in his thoughts. His dad had said something at supper about how terrible the drive to work would be on Monday. His mom said she hoped the furnace didn't go out like it did the last time there was a snow storm.

Slippery roads and broken furnaces, Kirby thought. *Adult problems. Problems I sure can't solve!*

"If they don't cancel school, at least we can make some epic forts at recess," Marvin said.

"Hmm," Kirby murmured again. His eyes fell on the Golden W Hotel brochure he kept pinned to his bulletin board for business inspiration. He and his family had stayed there on a trip to Halifax two summers ago. *A problem, a problem . . .*

"Of course," Marvin continued, "The Bear will probably wreck all the forts and get them banned, just like last year . . ."

"Wait!" Kirby shouted. The wheels in his brain began to whirl. Kirby was onto something. He not only knew it, he *felt* it. There was a tingling in his toes. There was a fiery hunger in his belly. His hands were forming into tight, sweaty, excited fists. "Say that again, Marvin!" he demanded.

"Say what? About school being cancelled?"

"No, not that." Kirby waved his hand impatiently. Fireworks were going off in his brain. An idea was beginning to form. A business idea. Based on a *problem* . . .

"Snow forts? The Bear?" Marvin asked.

Kirby kept waving his hand.

"Forts getting banned?" Marvin said.

"YES!" Kirby exclaimed, joining Marvin at the window. "That's it!"

"I don't get it," Marvin said for the second time that evening.

"Everyone at school is going to want to build a snow fort, right?" Kirby said.

"Obviously," said Marvin.

"Right! And we all know what happened last year with The Bear."

"Yeah. The Bear kept stealing everyone's snow blocks and destroying stuff."

"And then?" Kirby prompted.

"Then the kids started

fighting each other for snow. There was an all-out snowpocalypse, probably the biggest snow war Huddleston School has ever seen, and — *boom!* — forts were banned for the rest of the year!"

"Everyone started fighting and forts were banned," Kirby echoed Marvin. He felt a smile dancing on his lips. "Sounds like a *problem* to me."

Marvin raised his left eyebrow, puzzled.

"What if we *don't* build a fort this year," Kirby mused aloud. He began to pace again.

"We'd be nuts," said Marvin matter-of-factly. "Everyone builds forts."

"What if, instead, we built a *hotel*." Kirby tore the Golden W brochure off his bulletin board and held it over his head. "A hotel made out of snow!"

"*O . . . K . . . ?*" Marvin said slowly, clearly confused.

"Think about it! Forts are meant to be battle zones. They get everyone worked up and defensive and stuff. That leads to snow wars and fort bans — just like last year," Kirby explained. "But a *hotel* is different. A hotel is relaxing. People will come to our place to unwind, to rest — *not* to fight."

"What happens if The Bear and his buddies wanna wreck it? Do we just say 'Stop. You can't. It's a hotel, not a fort . . .'?"

"But that won't happen in the first place," Kirby said. "Not if we do it right. A hotel will change the whole feeling of recess. It will change everything!"

Marvin shrugged and shook his head. He didn't look convinced. Checking the alarm clock on the nightstand by Kirby's bed he said: "Better get home." Marvin stooped down to pick up his hoodie from the floor.

"Okay. Just one more thing," Kirby said. He leaned forward and lowered his voice. "We can *charge*."

Marvin dropped his hoodie. "Charge?" he said. "You mean, get paid?"

Kirby smiled knowing he'd finally captured

Marvin's interest. "A hotel is a business, right? You want to stay, you have to pay. Problem, solution!"

"But what would we charge, Kirby?" Marvin asked. "It's not like everyone carries around sacks of gold at recess."

"Everyone's got *something* on them," Kirby said. "What about snacks? Trading cards? A few bits of change? It all adds up!"

Kirby studied Marvin's face as a hungry, eager energy coursed through his body. A hotel made of snow? Genius! Plus, Kirby would be a real entrepreneur running not just any business, but a *hotel* business just like his hero! Sure, his hotel would be made of snow, but William T. Williamson always praised people who came up with unusual ideas. He called it "thinking outside the box."

"Well, it would be cool to make a few bucks," said Marvin. "But I still don't see how it's going to stop The Bear from . . . oh," Marvin paused as something beyond the window caught his eye. Kirby looked out through the swirling snow to see the lamp in Marvin's living room window across the street flicking on and off. "Jeannie's doing that *thing* with the lights again," Marvin said, rolling his eyes. "Gotta go!"

"See you," Kirby said. He stepped over to his desk and grabbed his blue notebook and a pen. "In the meantime, I'm going to start thinking up a great name for the hotel . . . "

* ** *

Jeannie DaSilva kneeled facing the wrong way on the couch in her living room. She pressed herself against the backrest, trying to get a good look out the window. She squinted and peered into the night, past the icy white sheets of snow that were swooping over the street like ghosts on a phantom speedway. *That's a ton of snow!* Jeannie thought.

Then, spotting a figure bundled in a blue parka trudging across the street, Jeannie smiled to herself, satisfied. It was her older brother Marvin coming home from Kirby's house. He was probably very thankful for Jeannie's clever reminder with the lamp that it was time to come home.

As she watched Marvin push his way through the wicked wind, Jeannie could actually see the snow growing into towering drifts before her eyes. *Perfect snow fort weather*, she thought, imagining the massive structure she and her Grade 3 friends would build at recess starting tomorrow.

Not only would it be massive, it would be the largest fort they'd ever built — the tallest, widest, strongest fort in the whole schoolyard! Jeannie could feel her toes tingle as she visualized towering walls made of thick, impenetrable snow-block stacks. Marvin was always telling Jeannie that only the oldest kids at school built big forts. There just weren't enough snow blocks and space to go around. Then he'd remind her about Brewster Marks, otherwise known as "The Bear." He was a big Grade 6 kid who busted down forts, especially the ones that came close to being as big as his own. *There's nothing you can do about it, Jeannie,* Marvin would say. *It's just the way things work at recess.*

Whatever, thought Jeannie. *I'm gonna show you, Marvin!*

This year, Jeannie and her friends were going to build the biggest, beefiest, best fort of their lives. The Bear wasn't going to stop them.

No one would!

#2
"Choose Your Staff Wisely"

Magic Monday Morning was Kirby's favourite time of the whole school week. It was when Mr. Santiago allowed Room 15, Kirby's Grade 5 class, to work on individual projects related to their future careers and dreams. Kirby used the time to plan his business career, of course. Quite often Marvin would join him, too (as long as he wasn't working on the latest instalment of his graphic novel series about his ninja cow character, *Moo Man*).

That particular Magic Monday, Room 15 crackled and buzzed with colour and noise. Vibrant watercolour masterpieces were being painted on easels. A group of students in the middle of the room dressed as pirates were rehearsing a play. In the far corner, a girl sporting headphones pounded out her latest song on an electric piano keyboard. Paper airplanes soared through the air as the creators discussed improvements to their aerodynamics. Meanwhile, Mr. Santiago bounced from group to group, asking questions and offering his enthusiastic 'thumbs up'.

"Our hotel needs a *feature attraction*," Kirby said to Marvin and their friend Jeff Hinkle. The three boys sat around the orange-topped table by the bookshelf. Since Jeff was planning to be an architect, Kirby figured it was pretty wise to ask him to be part of their snow hotel project. After all, Chapter Two of *How to Make Something from Nothing* was called "Choose Your Staff Wisely."

Kirby flipped open his notebook to the sketch he'd drawn the night before. It showed a palatial snow hotel with tall, smooth walls, neat round holes for windows, a grand, wide-open lobby, and a dozen or so guest rooms. Above the sketch in bold capital letters were the words FROSTBITE HOTEL. (Kirby had thought up the name when Marvin was leaving his house, letting in an icy blast of wind through the front door.) Kirby rubbed his hands with excitement as Marvin and Jeff pored over his drawing.

"What do you mean by 'feature attraction'?" asked Marvin.

"It's something that makes a building unique," offered Jeff. "Like making one of the walls into a really interesting design. That way everyone will stop and look at our fort — uh, I mean . . . our *hotel*."

"Exactly!" said Kirby. "I was thinking we could build an archway for the entrance. A really tall one — like this." He tapped his black pen on the massive rounded arch he'd drawn above Frostbite Hotel's front door.

Marvin bit his lip. Jeff let out a doubtful whistle.

"I don't think it will hold, Kirby," said Jeff.

"We're not supposed to build anything with a roof, remember?" Marvin added.

"It's not a roof — it's an archway," Kirby insisted.

"Teachers won't like it," Jeff said. "They'll say it's not safe. It'll get banned for sure."

Kirby felt a flush of frustrated red come into his cheeks. He wondered if William T. Williamson ever dealt with annoying business partners. Still, he had to admit his friends might be right about the archway. And he sure didn't want Frostbite Hotel banned before it even got started.

Kirby sighed. "Fine. What's another way we can get people to notice Frostbite?" he asked.

Marvin's eyes lit up. He snapped his fingers. "I've got it!"

Kirby's eyes widened eagerly.

"My family stayed at this place last summer near a beach," said Marvin excitedly. "They had all kinds of activities for kids to do — races and competitions and stuff. We could do that at Frostbite! It would be fun *and* all the noise and running around would get people's attention."

Jeff was bobbing his head up and down, but Kirby scrunched his lips.

"Frostbite Hotel is a *classy* place, Marvin," said Kirby, thinking of The Golden W brochure in his room. "It's not really a place for kids' games."

"But our customers *are* kids," Marvin mumbled. Kirby ignored him and added a few more flourishes to his sketch.

"What are you guys doing?" asked Allison Leaman, who was looking through the bookshelves nearby. In her hands was a thick blue book called *501 Amazing Facts You Didn't Know*.

Kirby instantly pitched his body forward to hide his notebook. Allison always wanted to know about *everything*, especially other people's business!

"You're not going to be one of *those* guys, are you?" said Allison with a loud snort. "The 'no girls allowed' kind? That's so lame!"

This of course attracted Allison's best friend Cassidy Sinclair who could sniff out even the smallest injustice in Room 15. Cassidy was going to be a human rights lawyer. She didn't just practise on Magic Monday Mornings — she practised all the time.

"No girls allowed?" Cassidy said, shuffling up to the round table. "What are you guys talking about?"

"They're going to build something called 'Frostbite Hotel' at recess. No girls allowed!" said Allison.

Kirby, Marvin, and Jeff exchanged a look. Kirby straightened up. There was no point in hiding his notebook anymore. Obviously Allison had overheard everything about his secret business plan.

"We never said that." Kirby tried to think his way out of the jam. He didn't want just *anyone* becoming a part of Frostbite Hotel. Then suddenly, spotting Allison's book of *501 Facts*, Kirby had a flash of inspiration.

"Hey . . . who here has ever heard of a *concierge*?" Kirby asked.

Marvin, Jeff, and Cassidy all shook their heads.

But Allison, just as Kirby suspected, smugly stuck out her chin. "*I* have," she said. "A concierge is a person who works in a fancy hotel. He — or *she* — makes sure people get special things they ask for. Like a reservation at a famous restaurant. Or tickets to a play."

"Is all that in your big, fat fact book?" Marvin asked.

Allison rolled her eyes and continued: "A concierge can get people anything they want."

"Anything?" asked Cassidy.

"Sure! Like turkey and mashed potatoes with gravy at three in the morning," said Allison.

"Or a cheeseburger with no cheese," said Marvin, kicking Jeff under the table.

"A monkey to play chess with," said Jeff, kicking Marvin back.

"Anything!" Allison declared.

"So . . . do you want to be Frostbite Hotel's new concierge, Allison?" Kirby asked with a grin.

"Whatever," said Allison, clearly pleased.

"What about me?" Cassidy asked.

Kirby looked at Cassidy and knitted his

eyebrows together, thinking about what else Frostbite Hotel might need.

"How about housekeeping?" Kirby suggested.

Cassidy's face turned a weird shade of purple. "Housekeeping? You want me to be a *maid*? Just because I'm a *girl*? No, thanks. That's discrimination!"

"But maids are very important in hotels . . ." Marvin began.

"No, no, no," Kirby said quickly, cutting Marvin off. "I don't mean a *maid*, Cassidy. I meant, you'd be in charge of . . ." Kirby struggled to remember something he'd read in the hotel brochure. He snapped his fingers. " . . . 'Guest Services'! You'd be making sure everyone was having a good time."

"I can help with that," said Cassidy, her face a little less purple. "But I WON'T be a maid!"

"No. Of course not," Kirby said. He looked

around the table at each member of his new staff. This was going to be great! He flipped to a fresh page in his notebook and made a quick list:

* *Jeff — Architect*
* *Allison — Concierge*
* *Cassidy — "Guest Services"*

"What about me?" Marvin asked, his brown eyes scanning the list.

Kirby pursed his lips. *Marvin, Marvin, Marvin — what could he do?* "You could be the hotel's odd job guy," he said, slapping the table. "You like building and fixing stuff. It's perfect!"

"Fine," Marvin grumbled. He didn't look impressed. "What's *your* job, Kirby?"

"I'm the CEO," said Kirby with a wide smile.

"What does that stand for?" asked Cassidy.

"'Boss'," muttered Marvin.

"*C-E-O — Chief Executive Officer.* I make sure that everyone and everything is working together. William T. Williamson says it's like being the conductor of an orchestra!" Kirby's voice squeaked with excitement. He felt himself rising out of his chair. He planted himself back down when he saw the strange looks his friends were giving him.

"Anyway," he said in a calmer, more business-like voice. "None of this is going to matter until we actually build Frostbite Hotel."

"Where are we going to build it, anyway?" asked Allison. "A lot of the best fort spots are already taken."

It was true. That morning, like any morning after a big snow dump, the students who got to school early enough before the first bell staked out all the really great fort locations. From the classroom window, Kirby and his friends could see the beginnings of several forts backing onto the schoolyard's chain-link fence. And though they couldn't see it from the classroom window, there was also the big fort by the teachers' parking lot known as 'The Den' that belonged to The Bear. Jeff had seen it, reporting that its walls were already waist-high. Of course, as usual, The Bear had grabbed the best location of all. The snow plows that dug out the teachers' lot after a snow storm always left behind 'The Hill', a massive pile of snow blocks. The closer you built your fort to The Hill, the quicker and easier you could create an impenetrable fortress.

"We're going to build Frostbite Hotel behind the portable," Kirby said, pointing to the small, shed-like building on the edge of the schoolyard. It was used as an extra class-room. "See? Marvin and I roughed in some of the shape before school." Near the portable was a series of long, skinny mounds of snow outlining the grand hotel rooms Kirby pictured in his mind.

"But that's a total 'no man's land'," said Jeff. "No one ever plays there!"

"Frostbite Hotel isn't a place to

play," said Kirby. "It's a place to relax. So, it makes sense to build it away from the rest of the action."

"That does it for Magic Monday!" Mr. Santiago called out, hands on his hips. "Books and supplies away. Let's get ready for recess."

Kirby slammed his notebook shut. "If you're all still in, meet me outside behind the portable." He pushed his chair back, stood up and looked at his new hotel staff.

"It's going to be *epic!*"

* ❄ *

Jeannie DaSilva, dressed in a pink and purple snowsuit and bright yellow winter boots, marched purposefully through the snowy schoolyard. She led a group of her Grade 3 friends toward their budding fort near the teachers' parking lot, right across from The Den. Though she was the smallest person in her class, Jeannie barked orders to the others like a drill sergeant. There was a lot to accomplish during the short morning recess and Jeannie wouldn't dream of wasting a minute of it.

"Ben — you keep working on the wall with the doorway. Selena — you can build the inside walls."

Turning to her best friends, Maggie and George, Jeannie said: "Let's get more blocks for our stockpile."

Jeannie knew, like every fort-building expert, that one of the smartest things you could do was grab extra blocks and make a stockpile. If you only took the blocks you needed and started building, there'd be no more blocks left on The Hill to finish your fort. It was one of the best fort-building tips that Jeannie's older brother Marvin had ever shared with her.

Maggie and George shifted anxiously in their snow boots. "Uh . . . didn't we get enough blocks before school?" Maggie asked.

"We hardly have any yet," Jeannie said. "We have to go back to The Hill to get some more.

Come on!"

"But . . ." George gulped, pointing toward The Hill. "Look!"

Jeannie, Maggie, and George looked in the direction of The Hill. Dozens of kids were scrambling all over its surface, grabbing blocks to haul back to their forts. They were mostly Grade 5 and 6 kids — huge, fast, and strong. A few of them may have been in Grade 4. There were definitely no Grade 3s.

"Can't we just use the blocks we have?" Maggie squeaked.

"No!" barked Jeannie. She looked at her friends and sighed. "No one's going to touch us, if that's what you're thinking. They'd better watch it if they try!" Tiny Jeannie creased her eyebrows and shook her fist in the air.

Maggie and George were still frozen in place, eyes wide.

Before Jeannie could say more, Ben's voice pierced the air: "*JEEEA-NNNIE!*"

Jeannie, Maggie, and

George rushed toward the fort where Ben was standing.

"Look!" Ben cried.

Jeannie looked at the far side of the fort. "No!" she gasped. The whole far wall was gone. The blocks weren't lying there in a heap. The wall hadn't fallen over. It was simply . . . *gone!*

"Someone took the stockpile, too!" said Maggie. Everyone gasped and groaned and started talking at once. They stared at the little hedge of snow they had propped up around the now-missing stockpile, to make other kids "Keep Out." Except somebody hadn't "Kept Out." And that someone was obviously . . .

"The Bear!" said Jeannie through tightly clenched teeth. Her eyes flashed. She whirled around to face the large, craggy fort that was beginning to emerge next to The Hill, the one everyone called The Den. The building had barely started, but it was already looking big and brawny. *All thanks to our blocks!* thought Jeannie, seething with rage.

Jeannie crossed her arms and stomped her foot. Then, with a fierce nod of her head she declared: "I'm going over there!"

To everyone's horror, she marched away from their fort all alone, heading straight for The Den.

"No!" cried Selena. "They'll squash you!" called Ben.

Maggie and George ran after her and grabbed her arms, but Jeannie shook them off. "I have to get our blocks back," she declared as she tramped toward The Den.

Before she got very far, Jeannie heard a commotion behind her. She whipped around to see two large Grade 6 boys beside her fort. They'd come out of nowhere, and were helping themselves to armloads of snow blocks. *Her* snow blocks!

Quick as a cheetah, Jeannie sprinted back to her Grade 3 fort. "Put those down!" she shouted. "That's our snow!" She ignored the cries of her friends who ran after her.

Jeannie stopped a few metres away from the

two boys. She planted her feet firmly and stared up into their faces.

"*That's . . . our . . . SNOW!*" Jeannie spoke each word slowly. She glared so hard at the boys that if her eyes had been lasers, they would have turned into two Grade 6 piles of ash. One of the boys was Seth Baron. He'd been friends with Marvin last year — Jeannie remembered him coming to her brother's birthday party. Marvin wasn't friends with him anymore since Seth started hanging around The Bear. Jeannie didn't recognize the other boy, who was wearing a toque with an angry-looking shark sewn onto it.

Seth laughed. "*Your* snow?" he said, turning to Shark Toque. "Hey, Darian — they own the sky!"

Jeannie clenched her fingers. "Put the blocks down!"

"Gonna make us?" said Shark Toque with a mocking grin. He lunged toward Jeannie and her friends, as though he was going to bite them. Jeannie's friends cowered back. Shark Toque cackled.

Jeannie didn't move a muscle. "Put them down," she said. She stuck out her chin and added: "And bring back the other ones you stole, too!"

Seth and Shark Toque laughed hysterically.

"Do you want us to rebuild the wall, too?" Seth said.

Shark Toque lunged at the group again, flashed his sharky teeth, and laughed some more.

"Good idea," Jeannie said, standing her ground.

Shark Toque dropped his snow blocks to the ground and trudged toward Jeannie. He towered over her and scowled. Jeannie tilted up her chin and met his eyes evenly. Jeannie's friends slid in behind her.

"If you want to survive recess," Shark Toque said. "You'll let us have whatever we want for our fort."

"Don't you mean *The Bear's* fort?" Jeannie taunted. "You just do whatever he tells you, right?"

Jeannie's friends gasped and shrank back. Shark Toque was no longer laughing. He rushed at them like an angry bowling ball heading for a group of wobbling pins.

"Hold it," said Seth, blocking Shark Toque with his arm. He gave Jeannie a dark look. "I have a better idea."

Shark Toque stopped, but his face was flushed with anger. The cold air streamed from his nostrils like smoke.

"We're going to take whatever we want from your fort," said Seth. "And you guys are going to let us." He stared at Jeannie and the rest of her friends.

"Ha!" Jeannie laughed. "No way!"

"Really?" Seth said. "See that lady over there?" he pointed to Ms. Linney, the teacher on recess duty. She was retying the laces of a nearby Grade 1 boy's boot.

"She'll stop you!" George said, finally finding

a small, shaky voice. "We'll tell!"

"If you tell, she'll stop us," said Seth, glaring at George. "And before you know it there won't be any more forts allowed, just like last year. You wouldn't want that to happen, would you?"

Seth was right. It was pretty lucky that snow forts were being allowed at all. Surely at the first sign of trouble — *bam!* — snow forts would be banned for the rest of the year.

"You shrimps don't want to get blamed, do you?" Shark Toque was grinning like a Great White. "Recess wouldn't be too much fun after that. Especially for you."

Jeannie and her friends stared helplessly as Seth and Shark Toque made their way over to the fort that had had such a great beginning. The two boys loaded up their arms, laughing as they promised to come back soon for more.

As Seth and Shark Toque began to saunter away, Ms. Linney walked by, holding a couple of Grade 1 kids by the hands. "It's so nice to see all the grades playing together," she said over her shoulder with a smile.

Seth chuckled and Shark Toque flashed his toothy grin.

"Yeah," grumbled Jeannie. "It's awesome."

#3

"Roll Up
Your Sleeves"

Kirby stood in "no man's land" near the portable. He surveyed the work done so far on Frostbite Hotel. Somehow, he thought their hotel would look more impressive by now.

Much more impressive.

But we just started on it yesterday, Kirby reminded himself. *We've only had three recesses to build so far!* He recited William T. Williamson's business slogan to himself: "*PATIENCE. HARD WORK. KEEP GOING!*" Kirby swept his eyes over the crooked slope of the hotel's measly outer walls. He sucked in his breath at the sight of rooms that barely looked big enough for kindergarten-sized guests. He had to admit that he was already having trouble with the first part of the business slogan — *Patience.*

Of course, it wasn't just the lack of building time that was the problem. The other forts in the schoolyard were being built out of big, solid blocks of snow from The Hill. Kirby decided that his staff wouldn't use blocks; they would form Frostbite Hotel with snow pushed up from the ground.

"But it won't look like a fort," Jeff had protested.

"Exactly!" Kirby had replied.

Building without blocks seemed like a good idea at the time as Kirby planned Frostbite Hotel in his blue notebook. He kept thinking about all the chaos in the schoolyard last year over snow blocks — who had the most blocks, the biggest blocks, the best blocks. If Frostbite Hotel didn't have blocks in the first place, there would be no reason to fight over it, right? He and his talented staff would find other ways to impress everyone with their clever snow designs.

Unfortunately, at the moment those clever designs looked like a crooked maze of wimpy walls — the kind of walls Kirby might have built when he was five.

"It looks kind of . . . *lame*," Marvin said.

Though Kirby agreed, he didn't say so out loud. What would be the point? It's not like they could start using blocks now. Most of The Hill would already be ravaged by the other forts, leaving very little to work with.

Kirby sighed, trudged over to the hotel's entrance, and fell to his knees. He helped Jeff smooth and shape the snow into a decent doorway. After all, Chapter Three of William T. Williamson's book was called "Roll Up Your Sleeves!" which basically meant that even CEOs had to help with the tough work when a business was just getting started.

PATIENCE, HARD WORK, KEEP GOING!

Kirby told himself each time he patted another handful of snow into place. *PATIENCE, HARD WORK, KEEP GOING!*

"Hide us!" A loud voice suddenly cut through the air. It was Ricky Spitzer, followed closely by Nolan Lebeau, two Grade 5 boys from Kirby's class. Before Kirby could say a word, Ricky dove over one of Frostbite Hotel's low side walls in a flash of grey snow gear. Nolan, a blur of red, rolled behind the hotel, causing an entire section of wall to collapse.

"Watch it!" cried Cassidy, who had been building the now-busted wall.

"Is he still after us?" Ricky asked, peeking over the wall into the schoolyard.

"Who?" Kirby asked.

"The Bear!" came Nolan's muffled voice from behind the snow pile.

"The Bear is after you?" Kirby repeated anxiously. "Then get out! Both of you — now!" Kirby wasn't going to risk having The Bear show up and mess with Frostbite Hotel before it was even built.

"He said we were taking blocks from The Den," said Ricky.

"Then Seth and Darian came after us!" explained Nolan.

"Were you actually raiding The Den?" Marvin asked incredulously.

"We're not nuts!" Ricky said. "We weren't anywhere near his precious 'Den'."

"We were just getting some leftover blocks from The Hill," said Nolan. "We didn't know The Bear had already put his claw marks on every single piece of snow at school!"

Kirby watched Ricky's eyes dart around the schoolyard, as if trying to detect any trace of his pursuers.

"We're clear," Ricky reported to Nolan. He jumped to his feet and brushed off his snow pants. "Hey — this is a pretty sweet location for a fort, Kirby," he said, looking around. "It's a bit weird and out of the way. But it's a great place to hide if there's trouble — no one would ever look here!"

"It's not a fort," said Kirby, rising to his feet. "It's a *hotel*. Frostbite Hotel. We chose the location because it's relaxing."

"A hotel?" asked Nolan, emerging from behind the wall he'd toppled. "So it's going to have a bunch of rooms and stuff? That's neat."

Kirby smiled, suddenly feeling a bit better.

"Are you gonna charge?" asked Ricky, sounding like he was joking.

But Kirby didn't laugh. "Absolutely," he said. "How else can I pay my staff?"

"Can we join?" asked Ricky instantly, pointing to himself and Nolan.

"I'm sure we can find some jobs for you. But you have to help us build," said Kirby.

"Sweet!" said Nolan. "We could even bring over the blocks from the fort we started."

"Frostbite Hotel doesn't use blocks," Marvin piped up, "Right, Kirby?"

But Kirby bit his lip. He glanced once again at Frostbite Hotel's sad, droopy shape.

"Actually, Marvin," Kirby said slowly, "I think Ricky and Nolan have a good point. Sure — bring all the blocks you want!"

"How much do you pay?" Ricky asked.

"I won't know until we start making a profit," Kirby said.

"Cash?" Nolan asked, his eyes widening.

Kirby shrugged his shoulders. "Maybe money. But other stuff, too. The stuff everyone has on them at recess. Gum, snacks . . ."

"Used Kleenex," Marvin grumbled.

Kirby ignored him and continued: "I think that with a little *patience* and *hard work*, and if we *keep going*, Frostbite Hotel will be a huge success. And when it is, we'll all be rich!"

A few small cheers rose up among the Frostbite Hotel staff.

Suddenly, Nolan craned his neck as something in the distance caught his attention. "Look, Ricky," he said, pointing. "We're definitely clear!"

Across the field, Seth and Darian were facing off with a tiny girl dressed in a bright pink and purple snowsuit and yellow boots.

Marvin jumped to his feet and burst into a run. "Gotta go!" was all he said before taking off.

* ❄ *

"I can look after myself, Marvin," Jeannie said through gritted teeth. Her brother, out of breath from dashing across the field, was trying to wedge himself between her and Seth and Shark Toque.

Brothers — yeesh!

"Can't you guys find anything better to do?" Marvin panted.

"Can't *you*?" retorted Seth. Darian laughed, his sharky teeth flashing.

"*I* can think of something!" Jeannie said. She looped around Marvin and aimed a kick at Seth's shin, but Shark Toque shoved her away before her boot made contact. He didn't push hard, but it was enough to make her lose her balance and land flat on her rear. *Ouch!*

"Don't touch my little sister!" said Marvin. He looked down at Jeannie. "Cut it out! I'm trying to protect you."

"I don't need your help!" said Jeannie, pushing herself up out of the snow. She crossed her arms and glared at Seth and Darian.

"Go back to your fort, Jeannie," said Marvin. "These two are bad news. *Trust me.*" He turned to the Grade 6 boys. "Really, guys? She's just a little kid!"

"I am *not*!" Jeannie protested.

Ugh! Why does he always treat me like a baby? Jeannie wound up her foot, ready to give Marvin a good kick of his own.

Shark Toque chuckled. "She sure bosses you around."

"What did she and her little friends do to you guys, anyway, Darian?"

said Marvin, blocking Jeannie with his arm. "I knew you were *low*, but I didn't know you were *that* low."

"Watch it, DaSilva," said Seth. Darian smacked one of his gloved hands menacingly into the other.

"When you're *puny*," Darian said, almost spitting, "you can sneak around without getting noticed. And before you know it — *bam!* — you're hauling off someone's best blocks."

Jeannie watched Marvin's jaw drop as he looked at her. Jeannie just gave him a smug smile.

"I can't believe you took blocks from The Den!" Marvin said. Jeannie shrugged nonchalantly.

Marvin turned back to the Grade 6 boys. "Come on — they're in Grade 3. They don't know all the rules yet!"

Seth grinned. "How about you, DaSilva? Do *you* know all the rules?"

"What do you mean?" Marvin asked.

"Yeah," Jeannie said, sticking out

her chin. "Tell us what that means!"

"Shut it, Jeannie," Marvin hissed. Jeannie stuck her tongue out at him.

"Sometimes," said Darian in an oily voice, "with a bit of help, we might forget about puny kids and the puny things they do."

What was Shark Toque talking about? And who was he calling puny, anyway? Jeannie looked over at Marvin and saw him bite his lip.

"Think about it," said Seth with a jab to Marvin's shoulder. Marvin didn't move.

"Just don't take too long," Darian added as the two boys turned to walk away.

"Jerks," Jeannie muttered, kicking at the snow.

#4
"Create a Buzz"

"FROSTBITE HOTEL: GRAND OPEN-ING!" proclaimed the large, colourful poster board sign Kirby and Allison had worked on in art class. It was propped near the entrance of the wide, rectangular-shaped snow structure. After several recesses of scooping, patching, hauling, and smoothing, Frostbite Hotel was finally finished.

Almost, Kirby thought, sweeping a critical eye over the building.

Frostbite Hotel's waist-high walls made of piled-up snow were reinforced here and there by Nolan and Ricky's blocks (*Could be taller*,

Kirby thought). An entranceway opened up the hotel smack in the middle. On either side of the opening was a pillar of snow designed to look like fancy columns from an ancient ruin (*Jeff's idea — looks all right*). It was wide enough for almost any kid at school to walk through comfortably. A small 'lobby' greeted anyone walking in, complete with a 'front desk' where you could register and pay. From there, the hotel fanned out on either side into two wings — the left wing housed two basic guest rooms, and the right wing a large 'suite'. Cassidy had even shaped a couple of comfy 'chairs' out of heaps of snow inside the suite to add a bit of luxury. (Marvin had wanted to cut out some holes for windows. Kirby told him 'no', thinking the walls were too fragile.)

Overall, Kirby thought it was pretty good, or at least not bad. As CEO and the one with the vision in the first place, he was bothered by the things he hoped others might not notice at first. Like how the rear wall kept toppling inward no matter how they arranged the blocks.

Or how the lumpy floor sloped awkwardly in several places. Or how you had to step over the front desk to work behind it because of the way the inside walls squished together. Size was an issue, and while no customer would ever know unless they were told, there were only about half as many rooms as the number Kirby had planned in his notebook.

Not that they had any customers — which was the worst problem of all.

"Where *is* everybody?" wailed Cassidy.

"They'll come," said Kirby to his staff, with more confidence than he was feeling. He wondered if William T. Williamson felt jittery whenever he opened a brand new hotel.

"I'm bored!" Ricky added, lying flat on his back, his legs propped up against one of the outside walls. He twitched his feet, causing three blocks to shake loose and tumble down.

"Watch it!" Jeff gasped, rushing over to make a frantic repair.

Kirby closed his eyes and pictured page 53 of *How to Make Something from Nothing*.

It was where William T. Williamson shared his top considerations when planning to open a new 'Golden W' hotel. PICK A GREAT LOCATION! and CREATE A BUZZ! were the first two items on the list. Kirby was sure they had a perfect location for a hotel by the portable. Out there at the edge of the school-yard, it was quiet, out-of-the-way, and relaxing. Kirby also knew that everyone on his staff had told at least two other people about the grand opening. That was what William T. Williamson called creating a 'BUZZ'.

In fact, the 'BUZZ' the Frostbite staff created was so big that some of the other forts in the schoolyard had started calling themselves hotels, too. This really bothered the Frostbite staff, but Kirby told them what William T. Williamson wrote in every book he had ever written: "COMPETITION IS HEALTHY!" Not only that, Kirby knew that you couldn't just call a fort a 'hotel' and be done with it.

Frostbite Hotel, with its planning and focus on quality service was sure to have an edge.

Suddenly, Kirby reached up and smacked his forehead. "FREE GIVEAWAYS!" he shouted. It was another item on William T. Williamson's list. Kirby had completely forgotten about it!

"MARRR-VIN!" Kirby shouted, running around the hotel. Marvin was patching cracks in Frostbite Hotel's left-wing wall. "The free giveaways! Did you bring anything?" Kirby and Marvin had hatched a plan on the bus ride home the previous afternoon to scrounge up some snacks from their pantries.

"Forgot," Marvin said with a shrug.

Kirby smacked his forehead again. How could they be so dumb? Of *course* FREE GIVEAWAYS were important. Who didn't like getting something for free? Not only did they not have anything to give away, they hadn't told any-one about them either. FREE GIVEAWAYS would have created a major BUZZ.

No wonder no one was here.

"Quick!" Kirby barked, whipping off his toque and holding it open like a bag. "Put something in here! A snack, a toy, a watch . . ."

"I'm not giving away my watch!" Marvin protested.

"Okay, okay. Not your watch. But cookies, an apple — *something*!" Marvin fished around in his pocket and pulled out a flattened bag full of crumbled cookies. (Or maybe they were crackers, it was hard to tell.) Kirby grabbed them, shoved them into his toque and ran around to his other staff members.

Ricky, still lying lazily by the side of the hotel, remarked: "I thought we were the ones making a profit, not giving stuff away."

"William T. Williamson says that 'sometimes you have to give before you get!'" Kirby quoted breathlessly. "Who has a pen or a marker? Someone write FREE GIVEAWAYS on the sign!" Kirby peeked into the toque. It was barely filled with Marvin's broken cookies (or crackers), someone's squished granola bar, and a half-eaten bag of fruit gummies. Kirby wondered if anyone on his staff lived close enough to the school to dash home and scrounge up more treats.

Kirby was about to ask when he noticed a pair of girls approaching. It was Dena and Maya, two girls from their class, dressed in matching red snowsuits with white scarves. They seemed to be heading right for Frostbite Hotel!

Is it possible? Kirby thought. *Could they be . . . ? Yes! They're definitely heading this way!*

"Customers!" Kirby whispered through clenched teeth. He swished his hands in the air, urging everyone into place. The Frostbite staff scurried into position either inside or outside the hotel, depending on their job. Kirby planted himself near the Grand Opening sign, on which Allison had just finished scrawling "Free Giveaways" in tiny letters with a broken pencil, and stood up as straight as possible.

"Welcome to Frostbite Hotel," said Kirby in his grandest, most welcoming CEO voice. "How can we make your stay wonderful?"

Dena looked at Kirby and raised her right eyebrow. Maya raised her left. The girls were known for doing everything exactly alike.

"This is your hotel?" Dena asked, looking the snow structure up and down.

"What kind of giveaways do you have?" Maya said, eyeing the sign.

"Gummies, cookies, granola bars — your choice. Would each of you ladies like your own room?" Kirby asked, then shouted, "Guest Services — Cassidy! Come look after our very first guests." Kirby could hear himself chirping and chattering like a monkey. He couldn't help it. Frostbite Hotel's first customers had arrived!

Cassidy dashed over to Dena and Maya.

"Follow me!" she said, guiding the girls through the entrance.

"When do we get the free stuff?" Dena said.

"As soon as you pay for your room," Nolan piped up.

Both Dena and Maya stopped in their snowy tracks.

"You mean we have to *pay* to get a free cookie?" Maya said. "What kind of rotten deal is that?"

"The giveaways are a bonus, but you still have to pay," said Ricky. "This is a business."

"What Ricky means," said Kirby, trying to keep his voice even. "Is that you'll get your treats as soon as you're settled in your rooms. Don't worry — you can pay us later!"

Maya snorted. "So we still have to pay. What a rip-off!"

"They probably charge a hundred bucks a day," Dena said to Maya, with a matching snort. "Forget it!"

"Forget it," Maya agreed.

The girls, arm-in-arm, marched away, their

red snow pants swishing in unison.

"Wait!" Kirby shouted after Frostbite Hotel's first almost-customers. "Tell your friends about us!"

Dena and Maya laughed the exact same laugh. "We heard that 'Brewster's Best Five Star Inn' has mini chocolate bars!" Dena shouted over her shoulder.

"*We* heard you don't have to give them anything at all," Maya added.

Brewster's Best Five Star Inn? Kirby felt his jaw drop. He knew some of the other kids had started calling their snow forts hotels. But . . . The Bear?

And why would a mean, cheating jerk like Brewster suddenly start giving away things for free?

#5
"Advertise in Three Places"

"It's all true," whispered Allison with her big book of facts in her hands. She settled in near Kirby on the floor during Silent Reading. "The Den is now 'Brewster's Best Five Star Inn'. And they *totally* have mini chocolates!"

Kirby, who was trying to read Chapter Five of *How to Make Something from Nothing*, gritted his teeth.

Something was itching at the back of his brain. The Frostbite Hotel staff hadn't told anyone about their giveaway plans — in fact, Kirby himself had nearly forgotten about it! And not only that, while The Bear was notorious for his fort-busting ways, he wasn't exactly known for being generous. Giving stuff away seemed like the most un-Bear-like idea in the universe! Kirby slammed his book shut with an anxious snap.

"Something wrong?" asked Mr. Santiago, who was at his desk looking over Room 15's projects on Arctic animals.

"Uh, nothing," said Kirby, sheepishly opening up his book. A few kids in the class giggled. Kirby had a habit of getting lost in his thoughts now and then, especially when they were about business. He felt his face turn red.

Kirby tried shutting out the rest of the class and his own irritation at The Bear by burying his nose once more in Chapter Five — "Advertise in Three Places."

In order for your business to be a big success, wrote William T. Williamson, *people need to hear about it in three different ways. For example, if someone sees a glossy ad for a new business in a magazine, then they watch a commercial for that same business on TV, and then they hear about it again on the radio, it starts to seep into his or her brain. Once it's in the brain, a person starts to feel interested. Once a person is interested, he or she is very likely to become a customer!*

Kirby closed his eyes and concentrated on different ways that he could advertise Frostbite Hotel to the students at school. A dozen ideas popped into his head. The trouble was, he needed to advertise fast if he wanted to get his business off the ground, especially with The Bear now running his own hotel. Where would Kirby find the time?

Pffffffffttt . . . screeeeeeeeee-chhh!

A piercing sound shot out from the speaker on the wall underneath the classroom clock.

"*Excuse the interruption,*" came the pinchy-nosed voice of the school secretary. "*The temperature has dropped to -31 with the wind chill. Lunch recess will be indoors.*"

Half of the students hooted and clapped while the other half groaned.

Kirby was suddenly sporting a very wide grin. *Indoor recess — bonus time!*

* * *

"Marvin! Where've you been?" chirped Kirby. It was the last half of indoor recess and a wound-up Kirby was sitting at the orange-topped table with a pen and his blue notebook. Marvin slid into the empty chair beside him.

"Just doing stuff," Marvin said, shrugging. "What's up?"

"We figured out the three ways we're going to advertise Frostbite Hotel."

"Why does it have to be three ways?" asked Marvin.

"Because," replied Kirby, "it works! It seeps into the brain . . . or something like that." He didn't know the exact answer. What Kirby did know was that if advertising in three ways worked for a triple billionaire like William T. Williamson, he was going to try it for Frostbite Hotel!

"First way — we're going to have brochures." Kirby gestured to the table beside them. He and Marvin leaned over and watched

Allison, Nolan, and Cassidy at work like an assembly line. Allison was making drawings of Frostbite Hotel with an icy-blue pencil crayon. Nolan took her finished drawings and above them wrote the top three reasons staying at Frostbite Hotel was great. Then Cassidy took Nolan's papers and folded each one into three neat sections to make them look more like real brochures.

"Second way — we're making a commercial," said Kirby.

"A commercial?" asked Marvin, wide-eyed. "Recorded and everything?"

"Well, maybe someday. When we have more time," said Kirby. "For now, we're just going to act it out for the class. I'm going to ask Mr. Santiago if we can do it right after recess."

Kirby pointed to the far corner of the room where Ricky stood clutching his arms around his body. He was clacking his teeth and acting as though he was freezing to death. Jeff was lying on the floor, arms propped behind his head and stretched out in perfect comfort. He delivered a huge, smiling yawn and looked as warm as a piece of toast.

"So, Jeff is supposed to be at Frostbite Hotel?" guessed Marvin. "And Ricky isn't?"

Kirby and Marvin watched as Ricky made a choking noise, clutched his throat, and then fell dramatically to the floor. He stuck his legs straight up in the air, stiff as icicles.

"Exactly!" Kirby said with a grin.

"Hey — can I be part of the commercial?" asked Marvin.

"There are only two roles in it, Marvin."

"Maybe I could narrate or something."

"We don't need a narrator," Kirby said. "But I do need your help for the third way. That's why I was waiting for you!"

Marvin's eyes opened wide and his cheeks puffed up. "Wait

— I've got it! We could do an announcement over the speaker. That way the whole school would know about the hotel! We could make it super funny, and . . ."

"I already thought of that," said Kirby quickly. "There's no way we'll be allowed to use the office equipment."

Marvin's face deflated. "Okay. So what's *your* big idea, then?"

Kirby rubbed his hands together, a glint coming into his eye. "Get this — we're going to get Jordan Enns to write a review for the newspaper!"

Marvin arched his eyebrow. "*The Grade Five Foghorn?*"

Jordan Enns was Kirby and Marvin's Room 15 classmate. Jordan was going to be a journalist, so he'd started his very own paper during Magic Monday Mornings, called *The Grade Five Foghorn*. Jordan worked on it every chance he got and gave out copies to the whole class each Friday. It had articles about school activities, sports, and weather reports. Sometimes Jordan even wrote stories about things that were going on at his own house. To Jordan, anything and everything seemed to be news, but Kirby wasn't sure if he had ever written a review. That was why he needed Marvin's help.

"You already have an 'in' with the paper, Marvin," Kirby explained. Marvin sometimes made *Moo Man* comic strips for the *Foghorn*. "Come help me convince Jordan that Frostbite Hotel is breaking news!"

"But . . ." Marvin protested as Kirby grabbed him by the arm. ". . . does anybody even read that thing?"

"Enough people will see it," Kirby insisted. "I'm sure it will seep into enough brains to get things started. Come on!"

Kirby dragged Marvin over to the computer by Mr. Santiago's desk where Jordan was busily working on his latest newspaper article. Kirby noticed the words *BIGGEST BLIZZARD BLASTS OF ALL TIME!* typed at the top of the screen. He also saw Jordan's bright orange memory key sticking out of the computer. The words TOP SECRET were scrawled on it in thick black marker ink.

"Hey, Jordan! We have a big story for your paper."

Jordan swung around in his chair, shielding the computer screen from Kirby and Marvin with his body.

"I'm listening," Jordan said.

"How would you like to write a review of Frostbite Hotel?" Kirby said.

"What's that?" asked Jordan.

Kirby's mouth fell open. Hadn't Jordan, of all people, heard the big BUZZ?

"You know — our snow hotel," Marvin said.

"Oh, *that*," Jordan said, sounding unimpressed. He twirled his chair back around to face the computer "So you made a snow fort. Big whoop."

Kirby threw his hands in the air. "It's not at all like a fort!" he insisted. "It's a *hotel* . . . and it's *relaxing* . . . and *fun*. There's room service and snacks. And as our guest, you'd even get to stay for *free*! All you have to do is write a review for the *Foghorn*."

Jordan stopped typing and chewed his lip as though thinking it over.

"All you want is for me to write a review?" Jordan asked slowly.

"Yup," said Kirby.

"And I get snacks?"

"Anything you want!" Kirby promised.

Jordan leaned toward his computer screen and scrolled through the open document. Kirby could see Jordan's lips move as he counted the number of lines he'd typed.

"I have enough space for a short article," Jordan said. "I guess I'll do it."

"Great! If outdoor recess is back on tomorrow, you are Frostbite Hotel's honoured guest!"

❄ ❄ ❄

Jeannie puffed out a breath of frosty air. She was scooping up mittenfuls of snow from the ground and patching up gaps in the snowy wall before her.

It had warmed up a bit since lunch, and last recess was outdoors again. "*YES!*" Jeannie had shrieked out loud as the announcement had blasted over the classroom speaker. She and her friends could get back on track with fort building!

That is, *hotel* building. All the older kids at Huddleston were suddenly building 'snow hotels,' not forts. In fact, whenever Marvin got together with his friend Kirby at Jeannie's house, 'Frostbite Hotel' was all they ever seemed to talk about. Jeannie was not about to be left out of the trend. She convinced her friends to transform their Grade 3 fort into 'Room 9's Super Hotel.'

"How are the towers coming along?" Jeannie called over her shoulder to Maggie and George.

No one replied. Jeannie turned around and headed for the free-standing snow block towers she had instructed Maggie and George to work on. She wanted her hotel to have a pair of pointy columns rising like two jagged dinosaur teeth in front of its entrance. Just like the ones in front of The Den.

When Jeannie got to the tower-building site, it was only half-finished and nobody was there. She heard voices drifting out from inside the Grade 3 snow building and headed in that direction. She stuck her head through the doorway.

Maggie and George were standing in the middle of the hotel 'lobby.' "Welcome to Mexico!" Maggie was saying to George. "Would you like a room with a view of the ocean?"

"What are you guys doing?" Jeannie interrupted.

"Playing hotel," said George with a grin. "Selena and Ben are out in the pool!"

"We're pretending this is Mexico," Maggie explained. "Ms. Linney thought it was funny."

"It's warming us up, too!" added George.

Jeannie rolled her eyes.

Playing hotel?

Being all cute and funny for the recess duty teacher?

Puh-lease!

"We're not supposed to be goofing around," she scolded, her voice squeaking in frustration. "We're supposed to be *building* a hotel!"

"We did," said George, looking at the spacious interior of the snow hotel. "There's room for all of us in here."

"It's the biggest fort we've ever made," Maggie added.

"Well, it's not big enough!" Jeannie said. She stomped her foot, causing a minor avalanche to tumble down from one of the walls. *It's not strong enough either*, she thought.

"Have you seen how big The Den is? Come here!" Jeannie turned and took a few steps away from the Grade 3 snow hotel. Maggie and George emerged reluctantly from the lobby.

"Look — it's *epic*!" Jeannie, pointing, declared.

Not far from Jeannie's Grade 3 hotel near the dwindling Hill rose Brewster's Best Five Star Inn. Built entirely of snow blocks, the main part of the former Den was a circular shape with walls taller than most kids at Huddleston. The narrow entrance was guarded by a pair of big Grade 6 kids. Snow-block corridors shot out from the main part of "The Inn" like tentacles or spider legs. They connected the main area to a network of smaller chambers. Even though it was a work in progress, it was by far the biggest snow structure in the whole school-yard. As much as Jeannie couldn't stand The Bear and his troop of sharky friends, she had to admit — they sure could *build*.

"Ours is pretty good, too. It's bigger than a bunch of the hotels!" said George defensively. "And we're only in Grade 3."

"What does being in Grade 3 have to do with it?" Jeannie demanded. "Why can't we make something big like that?" She jabbed her mitt toward The Den. "We could add hallways and extra rooms and super tall towers. We just have to work at it!"

"But what if The Bear thinks we're copying him?" asked Maggie. "Won't that make him mad?"

"No one from The Den has even come near us lately," Jeannie said.

"That's because your brother scared off Seth and Shark Toque that time!" George argued.

Jeannie threw back her head and laughed. "Marvin? Ha!" she said. "Seth was ready to give Marvin a knuckle sandwich!"

"But he didn't!" argued George. "Marvin must have done something. He talked to those guys, and then they left us alone."

Jeannie grabbed the ear flaps of her toque and yanked them down in frustration. "Marvin was just butting in. He didn't *do* anything! I had the situation covered already. Those big jerks just left on their own."

"What if they start bugging us again and Marvin isn't around?" Maggie asked.

Jeannie kicked at the ground, sending a thick spray of snow into the air.

"None of that is going to happen!" she cried. "The Bear and his friends don't rule recess. Now let's get back to those towers — *yeesh*!"

#6
"An Obstacle Is Just a Challenge"

It was a few minutes before first recess on Friday morning. Mr. Santiago had just told Jordan he could distribute *The Grade Five Foghorn*. Kirby leaped up and grabbed a copy out of Jordan's hands. "Come on!" He gestured to his staff. He couldn't remember ever being so excited to read Jordan's paper.

With his staff members peering over his shoulder, Kirby scanned the headlines:
BIGGEST BLIZZARD BLASTS OF ALL TIME!
ENNS FAMILY RENOVATES BASEMENT: MOVIE SCREEN ON ITS WAY?
THE HUDDLESTON SPORTS REPORT

"Where is it?" Kirby muttered, flipping over the page, then the next page . . .

"There!" Allison said, jabbing at the paper.

Aha!

"SNOW HOTEL HAS FUN, CHARM — AND FREE ADMISSION!" Kirby read out loud. "What? 'Free Admission'? That was just for Jordan. Now everyone is going to think you don't have to pay!"

"Um, Kirby," said Jeff, his eyes flicking back and forth over the page. "It gets worse. Look!"

Kirby read the next line of the review and his stomach did a somersault. Jordan hadn't made a mistake about the free admission after all. That's because Jordan's review wasn't about Frostbite Hotel — it was about Brewster's Best Five Star Inn!

The Frostbite Hotel staff started talking all at once about the article. *Why would Jordan . . . ? What would make him . . . ? How did The Bear get him to . . . ?* His friends' voices swam together in a murky cloud around Kirby's ears as he forced himself to read the rest of Jordan's review:

Brewster's Best Five Star Inn is a charming place to go at recess when you want to get away from it all. With its great location, there are lots of things to do, like building snow towers that become a part of the hotel forever. You can also help repair the hotel and really feel like you're one of the team. There are even snacks which you get to eat with the hotel's owner and his friends. Best of all, there is no charge, not like at Frostbite Hotel where you have to give up your snacks during your stay (plus it has a weird location by the portable).

Everyone should check out Brewster's Best Five Star Inn at recess. I give it Five Stars!

Kirby crumpled the newspaper into a ball. His knuckles turned a hot shade of white. He scanned the classroom for the two-faced reporter.

Where is that guy? Kirby thought. *Why would he do this to us?*

Last week during the special visit, the Frostbite staff had treated Jordan like a king. Kirby had made sure the hotel was whipped into perfect shape, and even gave Jordan the luxury suite to use. Nolan had snuck a mammoth chocolate cupcake from his sister's birthday party for Jordan's "room service" order. Cassidy had made a "Do Not Disturb" sign so that Jordan could enjoy privacy. Allison had even brought a selection of her mom's news magazines from home for Jordan to read. *It went on and on and on!*

Kirby began to storm across the room accidentally kicking over a chair with a loud clatter.

"Um, Kirby — come here a minute." It was Mr. Santiago. Kirby took a deep breath and went over to his teacher's desk. On it was a copy of the *Foghorn* open to Jordan's review.

"Frostbite Hotel. Like the 'commercial' you did for the class, right?" asked Mr. Santiago.

Kirby nodded, still too choked with rage to form words.

"It says you're taking snacks from other students. True?" Mr. Santiago asked.

"We don't *take* snacks," Kirby said, his voice barely a whisper. "It's our fee."

"Hmm. I think I get it, but you're gonna have to come up with a new plan," said Mr. Santiago. "Parents won't like it, for one thing. New plan, 'kay?"

It was too much. Kirby couldn't explain. He knew if he tried, he was sure to explode.

"'kay!" was all Kirby could manage to squeak.

❄ ❄ ❄

"Kirby, don't be crazy! I mean, you *wouldn't* . . ." Marvin said. He and Jeff chased after Kirby who was striding madly across the snow-packed field.

"Watch me!" Kirby replied.

As Kirby hurled across the yard, he passed rival snow hotels, all with signs just like Frostbite Hotel. (*Of course!* Kirby thought bitterly.) *Blizzard Bed 'N Breakfast . . . The Snowy Day Inn . . . Room 9's Super Hotel . . .*

Finally, Kirby had reached his destination — Brewster's Best Five Star Inn, as the sign declared in obnoxious red letters. He planted his boots in the snow and faced the huge structure. Marvin and Jeff arrived at his side a few seconds later, red-faced and panting. All three boys stared at the colossal 'hotel'.

"Whoa," Kirby couldn't help but utter under his breath. He'd spent so much time behind the portable, he hadn't yet taken a good look at The Bear's work. It was definitely the biggest snow building The Bear and his crew had ever made. Maybe the biggest in the whole history of Huddleston!

Kirby shook his head like a dog getting water out of his ears. He wasn't going to let The Bear or his massive hotel scare him. He had some business to get to the bottom of.

Kirby aimed his gaze at The Den's gaping entranceway, cupped his hands around his mouth and shouted, "Where is The Bea — I mean Brewster? I want to talk to him!"

Seth emerged from the

circular centre of the fort, followed by Darian in his trademark shark toque. Kirby sensed Marvin and Jeff shuffling backwards. Kirby stood his ground.

"I want to talk to Brewster," Kirby said.

Darian narrowed his eyes at Kirby, then went back into The Den. Seth stayed outside with a nasty smile on his lips.

For a long time, nothing happened. Then, a bulky figure darkened the doorway. He was at least a head taller than Seth and Darian, two of the biggest Grade 6s in the whole school. Brewster Marks, in his bulky black puffer parka, black ski pants, and enormous black boots really did look like a carnivorous black bear in need of a snack.

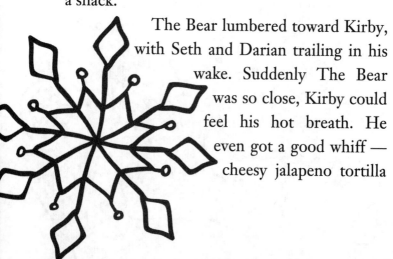

The Bear lumbered toward Kirby, with Seth and Darian trailing in his wake. Suddenly The Bear was so close, Kirby could feel his hot breath. He even got a good whiff — cheesy jalapeno tortilla chips. Kirby had to force himself not to turn and run away like a frightened mouse.

"You forced Jordan Enns to write about your hotel," Kirby accused Brewster, gulping down the nervous rattle rising in his throat. "You told him to write something bad about Frostbite!"

The Bear didn't say a word. He didn't move a single muscle except the ones in his jaw, allowing a sly, bearish grin to appear on one side of his face.

"Who cares about a Grade 5 newspaper?" Darian said.

"Come on," Kirby said. "You guys planned it. It's the only thing that makes sense!"

Seth and Darian began to laugh hysterically. The Bear stayed silent but was now sporting a full, beastly smirk.

"What made you think about asking for a review anyway — did someone put you up to it?" Kirby pressed, taking a bold step forward. "And what about the giveaways? Have you been spying on us or something?"

This seemed to make Seth and Darian laugh even harder. "We have our sources," said Darian. He and Seth high–fived one another.

"This is going nowhere," urged Marvin. "Let's get out of here."

But Kirby stood his ground. "You're not playing fair, Brewster!" he shouted.

"Boo-hoo! It's nawt faiwr! Wittle boy's afwaid of competition," Darian taunted in an irritating baby voice. A low rumble of bear laughter came from the depths of Brewster's parka.

Just then two Grade 4 boys, a tall one and a short one, exited Brewster's Best Five Star Inn and approached Seth and Darian. They were red-faced and breathing hard. Sweat trickled down from under their toques.

"We finished repairing the inside wall," said

the taller boy. He sounded exhausted.

"What about the towers on the outside? Did you get us at least five new blocks each?" asked Seth.

"Yes," said the shorter boy in a breathless voice. "*Six* each."

"The right size?"

The boys could barely nod their heads. It looked as though their necks had turned to rubber.

"Glad you enjoyed your stay at Brewster's Best Five Star Inn," said Darian.

Kirby's jaw dropped. *So that was how it worked!* Brewster's Best Five Star Inn didn't charge admission, but you had to *work* there in order to stay!

Of all the nasty, bearish ideas . . .

As the two boys walked away, Darian called after them, "Uh — wait up! I think you forgot something."

"Maybe we have to go visit *their* hotel to find it," Seth said. "Want us to 'visit'?"

The taller boy stopped in his tracks, then

turned around. He shoved his right hand into his jacket pocket and pulled out a Halloween-sized chocolate bar. He handed it to Darian, who handed it to The Bear. The shorter boy pulled a sandwich bag full of bright red ketchup chips from his jacket. They were crushed, but Seth grabbed them anyway, and passed them to The Bear, too.

"Thanks for the donation," said Seth. "And congratulations. You have earned a bonus stay at Brewster's Five Star Inn at next recess." His eyes narrowed. "We look forward to seeing you again."

They make you work and give them a 'donation'. Then they threaten your hotel and force you to come back for more! Kirby seethed at how The Bear ran his business. And to think *Kirby* was the one promising

Mr. Santiago not to take things from his class-mates at recess!

"This stinks, Brewster," Kirby dared to say.

Darian lunged forward, but The Bear held him back. Silently, The Bear turned around and lumbered back toward his Inn.

"Stinks," Kirby muttered again to Marvin and Jeff.

#7
"Team Building"

WHAP!

Kirby wound up with his hockey stick and fired a grungy yellow tennis ball against the metal garage door.

"Watch it!" cried Marvin who was playing goalie. Kirby's slap shot had just missed Marvin's left ear.

"Whoops," Kirby muttered, distracted. The ball rolled down the driveway, back toward Kirby's hockey stick. Kirby wound up again and fired. This time Marvin plucked the ball out of the air with his goalie glove. Kirby tossed his stick aside and collapsed backward into a snowbank near the driveway's edge.

"What's your problem?" Marvin asked putting his own stick down. He took a running start, turned sideways, and slid down the sloping driveway on the edges of his boots. He crashed into the snow beside Kirby.

"The Bear," Kirby said simply. "How did he get to Jordan?"

Marvin sighed. "What's the big deal? No one reads his dumb paper anyway."

Kirby sprang up onto his elbow. "It was one of our three ways to advertise, Marvin!" he said indignantly. "And what about the other stuff?"

"I dunno — a coincidence?" Marvin shrugged. "Maybe he's copying. The school-yard isn't exactly massive."

"But . . ." Kirby sputtered. "These are our ideas! And somehow The Bear keeps getting to them first."

"It doesn't really matter, does it?" said Marvin.

"Doesn't *matter*?" Kirby echoed, incredulous.

"Not really," Marvin said. "I mean — *we're*

still having fun, right? No matter what The Bear does."

"And now we can't even charge," Kirby said. "What's the point?"

"We can still try to get people to check us out," Marvin said. "We weren't making much of a profit anyway."

"Yeah," Kirby mumbled. "I guess."

Kirby flopped back into the snow in frustration. Nobody ever seemed to care about business plans quite the way Kirby did. Not even Marvin! He continued to fume over Frostbite's troubles with The Bear while Marvin tossed the tennis ball up in the air and snagged it with his goalie glove.

Maybe Marvin's right, thought Kirby. *Maybe the stuff with The Bear is just a coincidence.* Even if it was some sort of nasty spy plot, what could Kirby do about it? William T. Williamson always said that when it came to business, you should 'never worry about the other guy.' Instead, you had to focus on building an effective team of your own. In fact, just before Marvin showed up to play hockey, Kirby had been in the middle of reading Chapter Seven of *How to Make Something from Nothing*. It was called "Team Building."

"Hey, Marv — what could the Frostbite Hotel staff do together for fun?" Kirby mused out loud. "As a *team*."

"Why?"

"William T. Williamson says 'magic' happens to your staff when you do something fun together. You become better workers or something. He calls it 'Team Building.'"

"Oh. I think my mom did that with her work once," said Marvin. "They ran a 5K together. Or maybe it was a chili cook-off? She got a free T-shirt."

"Hmm," Kirby said. He leaped to his feet, picked up his hockey stick and plucked the tennis ball from Marvin's glove.

"We'll have to think of something," Kirby said, winding up his stick.

WHAP!

* ❄ *

"Winter Fun Day is coming up this Friday afternoon. Only a few more days!" announced Ms. Babick, Kirby's gym teacher. The students of Room 15, seated on the gym floor, bounced cheers and chatter off the walls like basketballs. Winter Fun Day was awesome. Not only were there cool things for the whole school to do outside, it was an afternoon out of the classroom!

"There'll be snow-shovel races and a toboggan pull like last year," Ms. Babick continued. "We're also adding snow sculpture making, and a new racing event — a snowshoe relay! We're going to practice that today."

More excitement bubbled up from the class.

Allison raised her hand. "Are we going outside?"

Ms. Babick shook her head. "During Wednesday's class, not today. There are lots of things to master in a snowshoe relay, like the proper way to run and pace yourself, and how to pass the baton. We're going to work on some of those team skills inside."

Team skills? Kirby's ears perked up at the magic word 'team'.

"We'll get outside with the snowshoes next class," Ms. Babick promised.

Another cheer burst from the class.

"Now, we'll need to get in groups of four . . ."

Groups of four! thought Kirby. *That's almost perfect! If only . . .*

"Can we pick our own teams?" Kirby shouted out excitedly.

Ms. Babick pursed her lips. "All-righty. As long as no one is left out. And I don't want to hear *any* complaining . . ."

Room 15 instantly began dividing themselves into groups of four by clasping arms, hustling over to one another, and calling out friends' names. Kirby urged all his Frostbite Hotel staff — Marvin, Jeff, Cassidy, Allison, Nolan, and Ricky — to gather round.

"This is awesome — we can make two

teams!" Kirby said. "We just need to grab one more person. Maybe Dylan . . . or Paige . . . or Riley . . . yeah, he's fast. Marvin — go grab Riley!" A chance to do some 'team building' had fallen right into his lap.

"Why are you acting so hyper, Kirby?" Cassidy asked.

"Because — this is perfect!" Kirby said. "Staff members who do fun things together are more successful in business. It's a scientific fact!"

Nolan groaned. "Why does *everything* have to be about Frostbite Hotel with you?"

Kirby felt his cheeks flush when he noticed a few of the others nodding in agreement with Nolan. But instead of getting mad, which Kirby figured wouldn't be great for 'team building', he tried a different approach: "Okay, guys. You're right! Not everything has to be about Frostbite Hotel. Let's just do something fun together as a group."

"Team Building"

There! After all, William T. Williamson didn't say that your staff had to *know* they were doing team building in order to do team building!

TWEEEET!

Ms. Babick blasted her whistle. "Okay, teams!" she called out in her booming gym teacher voice. "Gather up at the red line!"

Kirby led his Frostbite Hotel staff (plus Riley) toward Ms. Babick, a large grin spread across his face. Things were falling in place for Frostbite. He needed a 'team building' activity, and — *bam!* — the snowshoe relay landed in his lap. Not only that, the idea of Winter Fun Day was awakening new ideas in Kirby's brain! As Ms. Babick began a demonstration on how to properly hold the metal baton, Kirby's mind whirred and buzzed with new Winter Fun Day-style ideas for Frostbite Hotel:

Maybe Frostbite could host a recess full of winter activities . . . we could call it "Winter Fun Recess" . . . Oo! Oo! What about snow sculptures? That would be sweet! We could make a whole row of them in front of Frostbite Hotel! Kirby's eyes widened along with his smile as he imagined a long line of awesome shapes and beasts expertly carved out of snow. Talk about a feature attraction!

There was one more recess left in the school day — Kirby and his staff could plan a bunch of snow sculptures at recess and get started first thing the next day.

Only this time, Kirby vowed, *we'll make double-sure to keep our mouths shut!* This was one idea that would belong to Frostbite Hotel alone.

#8
"Expect a Few Bumps in the Road"

". . . and it should have five claws on each foot. Great big ones!"

Jeannie crouched by a heap of snow in front of Room 9's Super Hotel during the last recess on Monday. She was forming it into a snow sculpture with Maggie and George. On her way back from The Hill with snow blocks, she had seen The Bear and his friends making some sort of creature by their hotel. Jeannie instantly decided that she and her friends had to make a sculpture for the Super Hotel.

"How're we going to make him look like he's standing?" George asked, eyeing the uneven blob of snow doubtfully. Jeannie had just shared her idea to sculpt a ferocious polar bear perched on its hind legs, swiping its paws with beastly rage. At that moment, even to Jeannie, the shape looked more like a fat, headless snowman with puny legs.

"Does it have to be a bear?" asked Maggie. "I say we make a dinosaur instead."

"A stegosaurus!" George exclaimed. "With those cool spikes sticking out of its back . . ."

". . . and a spiky tail!" Maggie added with excitement. "It could wrap around the whole side of our fort and . . ."

"We'll use sticks for the *bear's* claws," Jeannie said, drowning out her friends' plans. "I bet I can find some dead branches in the snow at my house."

George and Maggie exchanged a nervous glance.

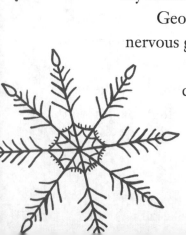

"But . . . a bear? *Please, please* can we pick a different shape?" said George, looking in the direction of Brewster's Best Five Star Inn.

"Why?" Jeannie asked, pretending not to get it.

"*You* know, Jeannie!" Maggie cried. "If we make a bear out of snow then the *real* Bear will say we're making fun of him."

Jeannie hid her smiling lips behind her pink scarf. Secretly, she loved the idea of poking a bit of fun at that jerk Brewster with a snow sculpture! *Maybe we shouldn't make him mean-looking*, Jeannie thought to herself, inspired. *Maybe we should leave him all lumpy and funny-looking, with weird, bulgy eyes . . .*

"The Bear will destroy our place for real this time," added George. "Or worse!"

"What's worse than that?"

George shrugged his shoulders. "I don't know. Maybe he'll kick our hotel down in half a recess. And then we won't be able to have a fort or hotel or anything anymore!"

Jeannie snorted and dropped on all fours. She pushed a thick layer of snow toward the sculpture with her hands. "No one's going to kick anything down!" she said. "When's the last time you saw The Bear or Shark Toque or any of those guys coming around here?"

Jeannie looked up at George and Maggie. They were both silent.

"I thought so," Jeannie said, dropping her head back down. "The Bear isn't the King of Recess, you guys. Stop worrying about him!" She began forming a clump of snow into a little ball.

"All right," Jeannie said. "Who's going to help me make the head?"

❄ ❄ ❄

Kirby was the first one to bounce off the school bus on Tuesday morning, followed by Marvin and Jeff. There were a few precious minutes left before the first bell of the day. Kirby's plan was to rush across the field to Frostbite Hotel and begin work on its very first snow sculpture. He'd told his staff about his top-secret snow sculpture project during yesterday's last recess. Kirby had opened his notebook and led a meeting for the rest of the recess to plan the best snow sculpture idea possible. After all, this was going to be Frostbite's big feature. They had to get it just right. In the end, nobody came up with a better idea than Kirby's first one — a pair of elegant swans, just like the stone ones that stood in front of The Golden W hotel on Kirby's brochure.

Kirby couldn't wait! He bolted across the field, full of adrenaline rush and ready to dive in when . . .

"*What . . . is . . . THAT?*" The words dropped from Kirby's lips like heavy stones falling into deep water as he came to a full stop.

"Looks kinda like a Sphinx," said Jeff, following Kirby's gaze toward the large, partially-formed snow shape in front of the entrance to Brewster's Best Five Star Inn. "You know — like in Ancient Egypt."

"I know what a Sphinx is, Jeff," Kirby hissed. It was all happening again! "It's a snow sculpture! Why is there a *snow sculpture* in front of Brewster's?" Kirby gaped at the snowy Sphinx. Then, he noticed something else out of the corner of his eye.

"Oh, no," Kirby groaned. To his right, in front of a different hotel, was a long mound with what looked like the beginnings of a pointed tail and a tall dorsal fin — a Great White snow-shark? To the left of the shark was some kind of boat, and to the left of the boat was a cluster of little snow animals, possibly rabbits. Whatever shapes they were supposed to look like, there was no doubt about one thing — they were all absolutely, definitely, positively *supposed* to be snow sculptures! Kirby whipped around and let out a yelp as his eyes landed on a trio of mini-ature snowmen, an oversized turtle, and what might have been a lumpy-looking bear . . .

"They're kind of cool," mumbled Jeff.

Kind of cool? Kirby slapped his mittened hands against either side of his face. He dragged his wind-bitten cheeks downward in frustration.

"*How did everyone . . . ? We only planned to . . . ? Nobody was supposed to . . .*" Kirby sputtered like a car running out of gas.

"Probably another coincidence," Marvin offered weakly.

Marvin and his coincidences! Kirby raged.

"Ms. Babick told us about snow sculptures yesterday. She probably told other classes, too," Marvin reasoned. "I guess everyone thought it was a neat idea, and started making —"

"You're telling me that everyone thought the *exact same thing* at the *exact same time*?" Kirby turned on Marvin and shouted.

"I could see it," said Jeff helpfully. "One hotel starts building a sculpture, then another one tries it out. Then another, then another . . ."

"Fine — I get it! But . . . but . . ." *It was a secret!* Kirby had been very clear about that. He'd made everyone on his staff take an oath of secrecy during the last recess. He'd even put Nolan and Cassidy on "spy patrol" to stop anyone from poking around as they made their plans. And no one had.

At least that's what Nolan and Cassidy told us, thought Kirby. He narrowed his eyes. What if they were lying? Or if not those two, what about someone else on his staff?

"There's a spy . . . in our group!" said Kirby to Marvin and Jeff. He jabbed his mitt in the air. "First the giveaways, then the review in the *Foghorn*, now the snow sculptures. Someone is giving The Bear our best ideas. Someone on our staff!"

"What?" Marvin's eyes turned into hockey pucks.

"No *way*!" said Jeff.

But Kirby knew he was right. What else could explain all the recent "coincidences" at recess?

"Expect a Few Bumps in the Road"

* ❄ *

"All-righty!" Ms. Babick's voice cut through the crisp winter air. "Quick review! Who knows what the 'anchor' is in a snowshoe relay?"

Allison, kneeling on the snowy ground near Kirby, began waving her arms in the air. It looked like she was trying to help a 747 airplane land safely in a blizzard.

"An anchor is the last person on the team to take the baton and run," Allison said with a smug smile.

"Right!" said Ms. Babick. "The anchor is very important, but so is every single member of the relay team. Now, before we get our snowshoes on, let's go over . . ."

Ms. Babick's energetic voice dissolved into a series of *blah, blah, blahs* in Kirby's murky mind. On Monday, Kirby couldn't wait to get going on the snowshoe relay prac-tice to team build with his staff. Now, even though Winter Fun Day was only two days away, Kirby couldn't concentrate on snowshoes. Ever since he'd said the word "spy" out loud, it was all Kirby could think about. It was the only thing that made sense! And if he was right, that meant that the guilty person was someone on his staff. Someone sitting very close by . . .

"Marvin, want to come up here to help me demonstrate how to pass the baton?" said Ms. Babick. Kirby watched as Marvin bounded up to the front of the group. Ms. Babick helped Marvin get into position, reminding him of the right way to hold out his hand to receive the baton from a teammate. Then, taking a few steps back, Ms. Babick began to wheel her arms and legs through the air as if running toward Marvin in slow motion. Everyone in Room 15 laughed.

But not Kirby. Kirby was too busy trying to spot a spy.

To his left was Cassidy sitting on her knees, twirling the end of her ponytail around her finger. Could it be her?

No, thought Kirby. Cassidy was a wannabe human rights lawyer. She was all about playing fair and sticking up for the little guy.

Not Cassidy.

Kirby turned his head to his right, his eyes landing next on Ricky and Nolan. They were shifting around restlessly in the snow, taking turns poking each other in the side of the leg. Each poke became harder and harder as they tried to get the other one to surrender.

Goofballs, Kirby decided. *Probably not great spies.*

Allison? Kirby wondered. *What did Allison care about most in the world? Being a know-it-all. Being the best at everything.* He could see it on her face as she watched Marvin fumble the baton during the demonstration. Allison had a look on her face that said: "*Ha! I would never drop the baton like Marvin!*"

But what did Allison stand to gain by helping The Bear? That would only make *him* the best! It made no sense.

Of course, there was Jeff and Marvin, but

that was insane. They had all been friends since kindergarten. Kirby had known Marvin even longer than that, since Marvin's dad and Kirby's dad worked in the same office and they lived on the same street. It was unthinkable!

But Kirby kept thinking and thinking. A strange picture began to form in his imagination — of a grade five-sized person, face covered in black, and dressed head to toe in a sleek black suit, like a ninja. Kirby squeezed his eyes tighter and concentrated on the image, as though if he just thought hard enough the mask would come off . . .

Like a big black spider, an imaginary ninja crawled across the snowy schoolyard in the dead of night, careful to avoid the shaft of moonlight that cast a beam down the centre of the field. Arriving at Frostbite Hotel, the ninja dug up a sheet of secret plans from beneath the snow. Rolling up the plans, the ninja crept toward The Den where The Bear sat in the dark, waiting for information. The ninja's head lifted slowly.

A hand reached up to the mask, peeling it back over the chin, the nose, the eyes . . .

"Kirby!" Ms. Babick's voice burst through Kirby's strange daydream. She and the entire class were staring at him.

"Uh . . . yeah?" Kirby said in a groggy voice, shaking his head.

"I said, do you want to go next?"

Kirby got to his feet and headed toward the practice space. He looked back at Jeff, trying to imagine him wearing a ninja mask. He couldn't see it.

"Here, Kirby!" said Marvin. He reached out his hand to give Kirby the baton.

Kirby, his body tense, his mind still churning, stared Marvin right in the face.

"What?" Marvin said, scrunching his eyebrows and leaning away as though he could feel Kirby's eyes prodding at his face.

Kirby felt his shoulders relax. Marvin was no cold-blooded ninja spy. The person Kirby saw standing in front of him was just his video-gaming, hockey-playing, snow hotel-building friend with the familiar goofy grin. What could Kirby have been thinking?

It was exactly what William T. Williamson said would happen the moment you started worrying about the 'other guy' — your business suffered, and you went a little nuts.

#9
"Faster, Higher, Stronger!"

Kirby stood in the last position on the course, the anchor position, his blood throbbing in his temples and right down to the laces of his snow-shoes. Huddleston students from every grade were gathered at the sidelines, jumping up and down in colourful snow gear. They filled the air with hooting and cheering and jumping as they waited to see the big snowshoe race between the last two teams at Winter Fun Day.

"ON YOUR MARK, GET SET . . . *GO!*" bellowed Ms. Babick.

Kirby watched as Allison, the first racer on "Team Frostbite B" took off. She had a fast, solid start. She kept her stance wide and her head up as she raced, just as Ms. Babick had taught them. But the Grade 6 team from Room 19 wasn't exactly hundreds of kilometres behind. This wouldn't be easy.

The race was the final event of Winter Fun Day. All the other teams including "Team Frostbite A" had already run their races. To Kirby's dismay, Team Frostbite A hadn't won (in fact they'd been clobbered!), although Cassidy, Jeff, Ricky, and Riley all claimed they had had fun. So, in Kirby's mind, Team Frostbite B *had* to win. First, Darian and Seth from The Den were both on the rival Room 19 team. But even more importantly, Kirby believed that if he and his Frostbite Hotel staff were ever going to be successful, it had to start with a team win — *now*!

Go, go, GO! Kirby cast urgent mind-waves through the wintry air toward Allison. *We've got to get this thing done!* Kirby

pumped his snowshoes up and down to get the blood circulating in his feet.

Allison approached Nolan at top speed, extending the baton forward. Nolan, hand extended behind him like a pro, nabbed the baton and was off like a jackrabbit. A cheer rose from the students and teachers in the crowd as the race began to heat up the frosty afternoon.

"YES!" Kirby cried. Not only had Allison put a good bit of distance between herself and Room 19's first runner, Nolan was really quick. He easily outpaced Darian, and in a blinding blur of speed soon reached Marvin, the next member of the team. Team Frostbite B was in the lead!

Marvin grasped the baton and propelled himself forward. He pumped his knees up and down, slapping the ground like a drum with his snowshoes as he ran. Kirby stuck his hand behind him and crouched into position. He looked back over his shoulder and caught a glimpse of Marvin's red, puffing cheeks, and sweaty hair sticking out from under his toque.

He also noticed Seth gaining on Marvin from behind . . .

"FASTER, FASTER!" Kirby urged. *Come on, Marvin!*

Marvin picked up his pace, snowshoes slapping and flapping with fury, his arms swishing and pumping at his sides. He was getting closer to Kirby. He was only a short distance away. Almost within an arm's reach . . . and that's when Kirby saw the oncoming disaster. A tiny Grade 1 kid, dressed in a puffy parka the colour of a Christmas orange, was twirling absentmindedly from the sidelines toward the race course!

Teachers and students were calling, "Get out of the way!"

"Watch out!" Kirby shrieked as Christmas Orange twirled faster and faster . . . right into Marvin's racing path!

Kirby saw the scene as

though it was happening in slow motion: Christmas Orange stepped in front of Marvin and seemed to stop, spinning in place like a toy top. Marvin dug his snowshoes into the snow to put on the brakes. Seth, half a step behind, did the same and tried to throw himself sideways to avoid colliding with Marvin. Then — *CRASH!* — batons went sailing into the air, and Marvin, Seth, and Christmas Orange were a tangled pile of snowshoes, winter gear, and kicked-up snow!

Ms. Babick blew her whistle and dashed onto the course. She was followed by a few teachers and students, all calling out in a panic. For a moment, Kirby was frozen like an ice sculpture, his hand posed behind him, as though he was still expecting to receive the baton from Marvin.

"GIVE US ROOM!" shouted Ms. Babick as she helped pry the crash victims apart. In a few moments, it was clear that no one was hurt. There was a torn snowshoe strap, a small rip in a set of ski pants, and some shaken-up feeling all around, but other than that, no serious damage done. In fact, soon all the crash victims were laughing, even the little kid in Grade 1. As they got up, the crowd went wild with cheering. Even Marvin and Seth quickly slapped each other on the back before heading back to regroup with their teams.

Kirby reluctantly left his position and trudged over to where Frostbite Teams A and B had gathered. Marvin was in the centre, babbling about the collision.

"And then there was this little orange blob coming at me like . . . *ZOOM!* And I was like . . . *AHHHH!*" Marvin tumbled to the ground and re-enacted the crash as everyone laughed.

But Kirby wasn't listening to any of it. All he heard was Ms. Babick declare that racing was over for the day and that the last race was a tie.

There was no winner.

#10
"Time for 'THE BIG ONE'"

As Kirby flattened the snow in front of Frostbite Hotel during first recess, one word sounded again and again in his brain: *genius*! All weekend, after the "snowshoe-tie fiasco" at Winter Fun Day, Kirby had been trying to come up with something big, something huge, for Frostbite Hotel. If 'team building' wasn't the answer, Kirby had no choice but to come up with an epic idea like the kind William T. Williamson described in Chapter Ten of his book. Something that would really put Frostbite Hotel on the map.

And boy, had Kirby ever come up with something epic. "This is 'THE BIG ONE'!"

he announced to his staff, dramatically levelling the snow as though he were a human-shaped Zamboni machine. "We're going to build a skating rink! First we have to flatten this whole area, right up to the fence." Kirby waved his mitt over the large space to the right of Frostbite Hotel. "Tomorrow, we'll flood the whole area with water and let it freeze up!"

Kirby stopped pounding when he realized no one was helping. Still on his knees, he looked at his staff. Cassidy and Allison both had their arms crossed, shaking their heads. Ricky was kicking at snow, ignoring the whole situation. Nolan just stood there with his mouth hanging open. Both Jeff's and Marvin's eyebrows practically touched the sky. Basically, everyone was giving him a look that said: *Kirby — you've lost it!*

Well, William T. Williamson had written a whole book called *They Said I Was Nuts!* — so, *ha*!

"Fine," Kirby said, "If no one is going to help me, I'll just do it myself!" He turned back to his outrageously brilliant task.

"Er, you know . . . making a skating rink isn't that easy," said Jeff.

Kirby gritted his teeth. "Of course it's not easy. If it was easy, everyone would do it. That's the whole point!"

"This is a . . . pretty big space." Jeff gulped. "Pretty *huge*, actually."

"Plus, who brings skates to school?" Nolan said.

Kirby slapped his forehead. Why didn't any of his friends have the same epic business vision he did? "Fine. It's not a skating rink. It'll be an ice-slider — a 'Slide-o-Rama'! We'll flatten out a running path, then flood a big patch of ice at the end to slide across. No skates needed. Satisfied?"

"How are we going to make the ice?" asked Cassidy. "We don't have a hose or anything."

"Empty milk jugs. I've got it all figured out," said Kirby. He explained that if everyone brought at least one big milk jug to school, they could fill them all up with water on their way out the door for recess.

"Hmm," said Jeff, like he wasn't convinced.

"What now?" asked Kirby.

"Well . . . it's just that it will take a whole lot of milk jugs to make a big enough ice patch. Even a small one. Even a tiny one. Even a puny one."

"Okay, okay. We'll just have to find a way to get back into the school a few times during recess to fill up our jugs."

"This is *totally* going to get banned," Kirby heard Nolan mumble.

Whatever, Kirby thought, ignoring Nolan's comments and all the funny glances he was receiving from his staff. *He* knew this was a good idea. They'd figure out a way to get around any problems — they had to!

An epic Slide-o-Rama was exactly what Frostbite Hotel needed to make everyone flock over from Brewster's Best Five Star Inn. As long as they beat them to it.

"This is TOP SECRET. CLASSIFIED. UNDER LOCK AND KEY. Understood? This is our biggest deal yet, way bigger than snow sculptures or anything else. No one breathes a word of this to *anyone*. Got it?" Kirby barked at his crew. He yanked off his mitts to wipe the beads of frustrated sweat that were forming on his brow.

Everyone grumbled a reply, sounding more like a broken down car engine than an energetic business. Kirby didn't want to hear grumbling from his staff. He needed them to work like machines, starting this instant!

"Where are you going?" Kirby said to Marvin, who'd begun walking away from the hotel.

"I have to check on Jeannie," he said.

"Again?" Kirby asked. He swore that Marvin spent more time checking on his little sister than he did working at Frostbite.

"I'll be right back."

"There's no time. Recess is almost over!" Kirby insisted.

"I'll hurry!" Marvin shouted over his shoulder.

"You'd better," Kirby muttered. Didn't Marvin know how quickly and how hard they would have to work if they were going to make the first-ever, made-from-scratch schoolyard Slide-o-Rama in history?

Sure enough, mere moments later, the recess bell buzzed across the yard.

"TOP SECRET!" Kirby yelled as everyone dashed for the door.

As Kirby stood up, a brilliant idea popped into his head. The school recycling bins! They were probably full of things that he and the Frostbite staff could fill up with water. The bins were set up near the school's other set of doors, so Kirby turned left and took a shortcut across the field. As Kirby tramped through the snow, he wondered how many containers he could carry back to Room 15 by himself.

Then Kirby saw something that made him stop in his snowy tracks. Leaving Brewster's Best Five Star Inn were Seth and Darian. Following them was the big, lumbering figure of The Bear in his puffy black jacket. And following The Bear was a familiar blue jacket, a set of grey ski pants, and a pair of bright yellow mittens . . .

Marvin!

Kirby's first instinct was to rush over to help Marvin defend himself. But then he noticed that Marvin and The Bear were talking. Nobody was shoving or poking or even growling. They were actually having a conversation.

Marvin didn't need Kirby's help.

What is he doing there? Kirby wondered as he watched both Marvin and The Bear stick their arms out in front of their bodies and look into the distance, as though they were measuring something.

Like maybe . . . *a running path for a Slide-o-Rama?*

Kirby felt his stomach lurch. Marvin hadn't left Frostbite Hotel to check on Jeannie.

Suddenly, Kirby knew.

Marvin DaSilva, his best friend since before kindergarten, was the spy!

#11
"Keep Your Friends Close"

It was still dark outside as Kirby and Marvin stood by the stop sign waiting for the school bus to pick them up. It had been a struggle, and once or twice Kirby had almost blown up, but Kirby hadn't yet said anything to Marvin about what he'd seen the day before at Brewster's Best Five Star Inn. Or thought he'd seen.

Kirby wanted to be sure, and now he thought he'd come up with a way. A test, actually.

"I was thinking more about the Slide-o-Rama," said Kirby. "What if we made the whole area in front of the hotel into a kind of theme park?"

"A theme park?" Marvin asked, jumping up and down in place as he tried to keep warm.

"We could make benches to sit on. Little shrubs and trees out of snow." Kirby watched Marvin's face carefully as he shared the details of his new plan. "I figured our customers might want to relax outside as well as play games," he said, struggling to keep a pleasant, friendly tone in his voice. "Like they're on a real holiday."

"Sounds sweet," said Marvin.

The yellow school bus announced itself with the familiar screech of its tires. As it pulled to a stop in front of them, Marvin punched Kirby playfully in the arm.

"Hey, Kirby," said Marvin, his voice becoming almost shy. "Were you mad at me or something yesterday?"

"Mad?" Kirby interrupted, his eyes widening in surprise. "Why would I

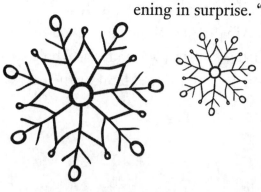

be mad?" *Here's your chance to spit it out,* Kirby thought.

But Marvin simply shrugged his shoulders. "I dunno. You were kind of quiet, I guess. And you didn't ask me over for hockey." He shrugged again. "Whatever."

"Right," Kirby said. "Whatever."

The door to the bus swung open with a squeak and a hiss.

"Hey!" Marvin exclaimed as he followed Kirby onto the bus. "If we're doing a park, maybe we could make beach umbrellas out of snow somehow. Or picnic tables, bird baths — stuff like that."

"Yeah," said Kirby as he followed Marvin into the bus. "Good idea, Marv."

Part One of Marvin's test was in place.

❄ ❄ ❄

It was time for first recess, and Mr. Santiago told everyone to get their gear on. Marvin was the first one zipped and laced into his boots, ski pants, and jacket.

"I'm gonna check up on Jeannie's fort," said Marvin. "Then I'll meet you at Frostbite."

As usual, thought Kirby. While coming up with the perfect way to 'test' Marvin, he had realized that Marvin was always the first to get outside at recess, claiming he had to 'check on Jeannie.' *Especially if there was a new idea brewing at Frostbite*. Kirby grunted to himself with satisfaction as Marvin took off, fast as a hockey puck slapshot. Today was no different, and Kirby was counting on it.

The bell rang and Kirby, followed by the rest of his staff, headed for Frostbite Hotel. When they got there, Ricky flopped on his back in the snow and announced: "I didn't bring a milk jug."

"Me neither," added Allison, looking around. "No one did."

Kirby noticed his staff exchange nervous glances. They were probably expecting him to go berserk. But instead, he shrugged. "This recess is too short to start the Slide-o-Rama anyway," he said. "I have a different idea."

He told them about his idea to build a park area in front of the hotel.

"We could make trees and stuff," said Nolan.

"What about picnic tables?" Cassidy offered.

Kirby grinned, hearing Marvin's own words from this morning.

"Exactly," said Kirby. "Hey — I think there might still be some blocks left on The Hill."

"You're not worried about The Bear stopping us?" asked Allison.

"Oh, I'm sure we'll be fine," Kirby said. "Let's go!"

The Frostbite Hotel staff marched toward The Hill, buzzing with ideas about the different things they could make for their 'park'. Their plans got more and more elaborate with every step. As the group approached Brewster's Best Five Star Inn, Kirby began to slow down his steps. He wanted to make sure everyone saw what he knew they would see when they looked in The Bear's direction. It was Part Two of the test . . .

"Marvin?" Allison was the first to stop in her tracks. She pointed toward The Inn.

"What? No *way*!" shouted Nolan, the next one to come to a halt. Soon everyone was standing with Allison and Nolan, staring in disbelief.

Until that very instant, Kirby hadn't wanted to believe it himself. But it was there right in front of him. Near the entrance to The Inn was Marvin DaSilva, clearly welcomed by The Bear and his jerky friends. He was even helping Darian stack a few small blocks into what looked to Kirby like some sort of chair or park bench . . .

"TRAITOR!" Ricky bellowed, kicking up a spray of snow. His shout caused Marvin and The Bear to look in their direction. Marvin's eyes became as wide as snow saucers, the kind he and Kirby sometimes took to the big tobog-gan slides at the park.

From across the schoolyard, the Frostbite staff could hear a deep-throated laugh coming from The Bear's shaking, bulky outline. He knew exactly what was going on. And he clearly thought it was all rather hysterical.

Marvin lunged forward and started to shout something, but The Bear grabbed him, pre-venting him from getting any closer to Kirby and the Frostbite staff.

"Don't bother!" Kirby shouted. "We don't want you, anyway!"

"Kirby! Guys!" Marvin yelled. "WAIT!" His body hung limply in The Bear's grasp.

Kirby gulped, fighting a sudden instinct to grab Marvin, head back to Frostbite, and forget about the whole thing.

Instead, he narrowed his eyes and sent back a silent reply to his former friend: *Serves you right!*

Kirby turned to his

staff. "Come on," he said bitterly. Together, they marched away, leaving Marvin with his snow-saucer eyes far, far behind.

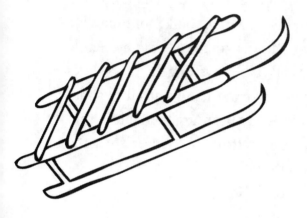

#12

"The Mirror Test"

"If you're finished your rough copy, you can share in groups," Mr. Santiago announced to the class.

Kirby snatched his creative writing paragraph and a pencil off his desk. He looked up, automatically scanning the room for Marvin. Just as the two boys were about to lock eyes, Kirby remembered to turn his face away. He'd been doing it all day since Marvin failed his 'test' at recess.

"Jeff!" Kirby called out across the room. "Wanna be in a group?"

"Over here," Jeff said, gesturing for Kirby

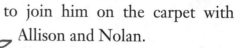

to join him on the carpet with Allison and Nolan.

The four of them shuffled into a small circle. They all faced Allison who volunteered to share her paragraph first:

"BOOM!" Allison read from her paper. *"The old, mysterious red clock on the blue dresser fell down and smashed into pieces . . ."*

Kirby felt something brush against his arm. It was Marvin, trying to squeeze in beside him on the carpet. Kirby shifted his body to block any possible open space.

"Can't I sit here?" said Marvin.

Allison stopped reading. She looked straight ahead, right over Marvin's shoulder. "Did somebody say something?" she asked, batting her eyelashes innocently.

Jeff looked around, careful to keep his eyes off Marvin. "Nope. I didn't say anything," he said. "Did you?" He looked at Nolan.

Kirby felt Marvin scooch closer to him. He angled his back to Marvin even more sharply, tightening up the circle.

"It's probably the wind," said Nolan. "Actually . . ." he took a few sniffs of air. "Does something smell around here?"

Allison tilted her nose in the air and took a long, dramatic whiff.

"Fine!" Marvin grumbled as he got up and moved away.

❄ ❄ ❄

On the bus ride home, Marvin didn't even try to sit with Kirby. He chose a spot alone near the front by all the younger kids.

Kirby sat in his usual bus seat at the back, the seat he usually shared with Marvin. He was determined to read *How to Make Something from Nothing*, even if he got carsick all over the place, which sometimes happened when he tried to read in a moving vehicle.

Thinking about business was one thing that might get his mind off the whole mess with Marvin.

Of course, getting carsick might be another way . . .

By now, your business adventure is well under-way! Kirby read, holding the book as steady as he could in front of his face. *Some days have been exciting, while others have been frustrating . . .*

Most have been frustrating! Kirby corrected. He continued reading:

It's time to check in with yourself, new CEO. It's time to see if you are still heading up, up, up, and away toward the BUSINESS STRATOSPHERE. Remember — there's more than one path to those dizzying heights of success! YOU want to make sure that YOU are on the right one. Here's a simple experiment that I think every good CEO must do as he or she grows a new business . . .

Finally, Kirby thought. *Here we go!* William T. Williamson was about to share something important. A juicy business secret. Kirby could sense it.

"The Mirror Test"

I call it 'THE MIRROR TEST'. It's quite simple. You don't have to study. You don't have to prepare. You've done all the necessary work already just by working at your business. All you need to do is look at yourself in the mirror and tell yourself 'I'M PROUD OF THE WAY I RUN MY BUSINESS.' If you can do it, you've passed the test!

Kirby let the book drop to his lap. *That was the big secret?!?* he thought. *I'm supposed to look in the mirror and say 'I'm proud of myself'? That's why William T. Williamson is a triple ga-gillionaire?* He slammed the book shut in disgust.

Kirby felt his stomach do a few somersaults from all the bouncing words. He pressed his warm forehead against the cold school bus window, catching a glimpse of his tired, frowning face reflected in the glass. Kirby quickly shut his eyes.

✳ ❄ ✳

The airbrakes hissed as the bus pulled away from Kirby's stop. Kirby looked down as he walked, and pretended not to hear Marvin and Jeannie's footsteps behind him as they headed for their house across the street.

Kirby was halfway up his driveway when he heard Marvin's voice.

"Wait up!"

Kirby picked up his pace.

"Kirby!" Marvin called out again.

Kirby closed his eyes, bit his lip, and slowly turned around. Marvin was standing across the street at the edge of his own driveway.

So this was it. They were going to fight. Better just get it over with . . .

But Marvin surprised him, shouting out: "I know you hate me, Kirby. But just so you know — The Bear is planning to destroy all the hotels tomorrow. It's over."

What? Kirby hadn't expected that. But he swallowed his shock.

"And you're going to help him, right?" Kirby shouted back. "Thanks for the heads up!"

"Of course I'm not going to help him," Marvin was indignant. "I'm telling you so we can protect Frostbite!"

'We'? thought Kirby. 'We' can protect Frostbite Hotel from The Bear?

Something in Kirby snapped. He dropped his school bag with a thud on the icy driveway. He stormed across the empty street. He marched right up to Marvin who hadn't moved a muscle.

"Since when did you ever care about Frostbite?" Kirby lashed out. "You've been a traitor since day one!"

"I'm not a traitor!"

"What do you call giving all our best ideas to The Bear?"

"It didn't stop us from using them . . ." Marvin began defensively.

"That's not the point and you know it!"

Kirby grabbed the collar of Marvin's jacket. He was about to toss him into the snow bank and give him the face-wash of his life!

"Okay! Okay! It was dumb!" Marvin shouted. "But . . . I did it to protect Jeannie, all right? I'm sorry!"

Jeannie? Kirby loosened his hand. *How did hanging out with The Bear help Jeannie? Unless . . .*

"They said if I gave them some good ideas for their hotel, they'd leave Jeannie alone." Marvin was still shouting, eyeing Kirby's grip nervously. "It was working, so I kept doing it. You know how those guys can be. I didn't want her to get creamed."

Kirby released Marvin, his blood still boiling. He tried to process the new information, but before either of them could say another word, a high-pitched, raging voice sliced through the air.

"Marvin, you big *jerk*!" Jeannie stood on the DaSilva's front porch. Her face was redder than a ripe tomato about to burst. "Why would you do that? I am not a little wimp. I don't need you to protect me — *ever*! I can take care of myself!" She yanked open the front door and slammed it behind her as she stomped inside.

"Oh, great," mumbled Marvin. He tossed his school bag aside and deflated into the snow bank.

Kirby stood frozen for a moment on the driveway. His urge to facewash Marvin hadn't entirely disappeared. He took a few deep breaths, then made his way over to the snow bank. He sank to his knees in the snow.

"Why didn't you say something?" Kirby asked. He flopped backwards beside Marvin.

"I dunno," Marvin shrugged. "It just kinda started . . . *happening*. I didn't think you'd get it."

"Still, if you'd just — " Kirby began, but he was interrupted by the creaking sound of the DaSilva's garage door opening.

Kirby and Marvin sat up and turned around. There was Jeannie, standing at the edge of the garage in her pink and purple snowsuit. Cradled in her arms was a bright orange bazooka water soaker nearly half her size.

"Jeannie . . . don't you dare . . . " Marvin gasped.

With a blood-curdling yell, Jeannie tore straight for Kirby and Marvin, ejecting forceful streams of water from the toy gun as she ran.

The boys shouted, rewarded by soaking wet jackets and mouthfuls of freezing cold water.

"RUN!" shouted Kirby.

"BACKYARD!" Marvin yelled to Kirby. Kirby scrambled after Marvin around the side of the house.

Kirby and Marvin ducked and dodged. They tried tackling Jeannie, then corralling her by the snow-covered deck. They ran behind a tree, then in separate directions. They flung snow at her. But Jeannie just kept coming after them.

"In here!" Marvin cried out. He dove over the wall of a big snow fort in the middle of the yard. Kirby took a running leap and soared through the air, landing beside Marvin. "Snowballs!" Marvin instructed, heaping handfuls of snow into defensive spheres.

"Too late!" Kirby cried out. There was Jeannie, a crazy grin on her face, peering over the wall, priming the bazooka for another blast. "Get her!"

The boys grabbed Jeannie's arms. She toppled headfirst into the fort. Kirby yanked the bazooka soaker from her hands and tossed it into the yard.

"You are SO getting facewashed!" Marvin said through gritted teeth as he pulled Jeannie into a headlock and grabbed a handful of snow.

Kirby, meanwhile, was looking around him in awe. "Did you make this fort?" he asked Marvin.

"No — *I* did!" Jeannie declared, still struggling in Marvin's headlock. "With no help from *him*!" She glared up at her brother with fire in her eyes.

"It's pretty good," Kirby said, nodding his head appreciatively.

"You're just saying that," Jeannie

cried, kicking and wiggling as Marvin held her down. "You just don't want me to soak you again!"

"No, I mean it," Kirby said. "Marvin — we never made a fort like this in Grade 3, did we?"

Marvin shrugged, but nodded his head.

"Look how *even* the walls are," said Kirby. "And the corners — *nice*."

Marvin relaxed his grip on his little sister.

"You should see Room 9's Super Hotel at school," Jeannie boasted, as she sat up and brushed snow off her snowsuit. "It's WAY bigger than this. It's almost as big as Brewster's Inn."

"Not quite that big," said Marvin, rolling his eyes.

Jeannie leaned in toward her brother's face. "It could be!" she retorted.

"Wait . . ." Kirby held his hand up in the air. He needed silence.

An idea was beginning to form in his mind . . .

"Marvin — The Bear is going to wreck all the hotels tomorrow, right?"

Marvin nodded. "First recess. Total 'snow-pocalypse' — just like last year."

"Right. Then everyone goes nuts destroying hotels, forts, whatever. And we're banned from making anything at recess."

"That jerk!" Jeannie muttered.

"Unless that's *not* what happens." Kirby eyed Jeannie's impressive fort, nodding to himself.

The Bear. Room 9's Super Hotel. 'Snowpocalypses' and the secret to avoiding them . . . Kirby's thoughts were beginning to come together like one giant, sticky snowball. "I think I might be onto something, you guys," he said slowly. "A way to stop The Bear. At least for now. But Jeannie, we're going to need your help."

Jeannie's eyes narrowed. "Oh, yeah? Why would I want to help you? And besides." — she scowled at Marvin — "I'm just a weak little kid, remember?"

"No way," Kirby said quickly, before Marvin could react. "You're a born leader.

Believe me, I've been doing a lot of research on the subject. And we're going to need you to lead a really important part of this operation."

Jeannie looked at him sideways for a moment. "Okay," she said. "I'm in. But no thanks to you!" She walloped Marvin on the shoulder with a mittened fist.

"Good," said Kirby with relief. He turned to Marvin, who was rubbing his shoulder. "Oh — and we'll have to let the other hotels in on it."

"I know some kids who have forts. Yossi and Rachel. Also Garnet, Mitchell, and Parker . . ." Jeannie said.

"Perfect!" Kirby clapped his hands together. "Can you talk to them before the first bell?"

Jeannie nodded.

"What is it?" asked Marvin, leaning forward. "What are you thinking, Kirby?"

"It's just a spark," said Kirby, looking Marvin in the eye, "but I think it can work. We'll have to make an emergency call to all the Frostbite staff — tonight."

#13

"Consider a 'Joint Venture"

BANG!

Kirby pushed the school doors open wide, allowing a blast of cold air to flood into the school. Jeff, Cassidy, Nolan, Ricky, and Allison followed behind him. It was first recess and time to put their plan to work.

Kirby paused for barely a second to cast a glance toward the portable and Frostbite Hotel. But this was no time to get sentimental. He, his staff, and virtually the rest of the school had work to do!

Kirby led the Frostbite Hotel staff in the direction of The Hill, looking as though they were only on a mission to get more snow blocks for their hotel. Meanwhile, Marvin ducked out from behind the rest of the group. He headed straight for The Den where The Bear was still expecting him to join in the snowpocalypse plans.

It was almost time to launch into action.

Almost . . .

Kirby and the Frostbite staff reached Room 9's Super Hotel. Kirby snuck a glance toward the nearby Den, where he saw Marvin leading The Bear out front, waving in the direction of the portable . . . and Frostbite Hotel.

Look, guys! There's no one there. No kids, no teachers! Marvin was probably saying, just as he and Kirby had planned yesterday in Marvin's backyard. *Let's start the snowpocalypse at Frostbite!*

Then, like clockwork, Phase One of the plan began. The Bear bellowed something at his gang inside the snowy lair. Seth, Darian, and the other denmates emerged and they all turned their heads toward Frostbite, like prairie dogs in the tall grass startled by a noise in the distance.

Suddenly, they were off.

The Bear went first, trudging heavily and purposefully through the snow, followed by the others. They were a threatening mob, stomping their boots and smacking their gloves together with glee, their hoots of triumph filling the frigid air. Marvin kept his arm outstretched toward Frostbite, urging them toward the defenceless hotel, though he himself held back from the rush. Just as Marvin had predicted, none of The Den members seemed to care whether he joined them or stayed behind. After all, Marvin wasn't really one of *them*.

As soon as The Den members were out of view, it was time for Phase Two. Jeannie, Maggie, and George dashed out of Room 9's Super Hotel right on cue.

"Ooh! Ooh! Ms. Linney!" said Jeannie, whizzing past Kirby and the Frostbite staff toward the teacher on recess duty. "Did you see the snow sculptures my brother and his friends made?

They're soooo pretty!" Jeannie was using her most little-girlish, sing-songy voice as she grabbed the teacher's hand.

Not like that insane warrior cry from yesterday, Kirby thought.

"They're the best sculptures in the *whoooole schoooool!*" cooed Maggie, batting her lashes. She and George play-fought over who got to grab Ms. Linney's other hand. Skipping and yapping like playful little puppies, Jeannie and her friends led Ms. Linney across the field toward the portable.

Kirby and his staff tried their best to look straight ahead as they walked, pretending to have no idea about what was going on around them. Out of the corner of his eye, Kirby tried to take in enough of the unfolding action to make sure his plan was working. A few moments later, he was satisfied.

"Okay, guys," Kirby said. He stepped up onto a snow-bench in front of Room 9's Super Hotel. He faced his staff and the schoolyard. "Phase Three!" he shouted, waving his arms in the air.

What looked like random clusters of students standing around in the schoolyard suddenly sprang to life. Near Room 9's Super Hotel, boys and girls from the younger grades began to form corridors of snow linking Jeannie's hotel to some of the other nearby snow structures. Elsewhere, the schoolyard had become a network of relays. Blocks of snow were being passed from person to person toward Jeannie's place with astonishing speed. Nolan, Allison, and Ricky were part of this system, delivering blocks and urging on the runners and carriers from the other forts. It was like a series of relay races, only with snow blocks being passed instead of batons!

Meanwhile, Kirby, Marvin, Jeff, and Cassidy were working in the trenches near Jeannie's hotel with kids from other forts, forming a mega-building crew. As snow blocks arrived at the Super Hotel, they grabbed them and began to expertly stack and arrange them, forming the existing walls into taller walls, thicker walls, and even brand new walls.

"*Have . . . you . . . seen . . . The . . . Bear?*" Kirby gasped to Marvin. The two boys were lifting up a huge block together and sliding it into place on the wall before them.

"*Not . . . so . . . far . . .*" Marvin panted back.

They worked fast — really fast. Kirby was huffing and puffing and heating up under his jacket. Sweat was trickling from under his toque and rolling down his cheeks. Kirby had never worked this quickly or this hard in all the recesses of his life put together.

"It worked! It worked! We got them!" A shrill, powerful voice burst above the grunting of the workers. Kirby looked up and saw Jeannie and her friends dashing toward the Super Hotel.

"We got them!" Jeannie hooted again. "Big time!"

Kirby and Marvin exchanged a look. They put down their blocks and headed toward Jeannie.

"Ms. Linney caught The

Bear busting up your hotel!" she shouted. "She sent all of them inside for the whole recess. WE GOT 'EM BIG TIME!"

Kirby and Marvin whooped in triumph. *YES! IT WORKED.*

Kirby dashed over to the bench and stepped up. He waved his arms furiously and shouted. "The Bear's inside! Snowpocalypse is off!" A cheer rose in front of Kirby, and more cheers erupted as the message passed from person to person.

"Hey, Jeannie," Kirby called out as he stepped down from the bench. Jeannie turned to him.

"What about Frostbite?" Kirby asked biting his lip. He knew the answer. After all, it was part of the plan. But he had to ask anyway.

"Gone," Jeannie replied. Kirby dropped his head.

"Big time."

* * *

The mega-building project continued through

the long lunch recess. The Bear and his crew were still trapped inside the school, serving out their punishment in the principal's office. Allison, who had made an excuse to go sleuthing near the office after first recess, reported that The Bear and his crew even had to eat lunch there. And not only that, if they so much as disturbed a single snowflake from another kid's fort, they'd have to miss recess for the whole week — maybe longer.

There was no denying it. The entire school was completely pumped by the successful trapping of The Bear and his buddies, but even more by the epic hotel they'd started during the short first recess. The snow colossus that rose before them, the result of a school-wide building effort, had never been possible before. Or at least, it had never been thought of before. But now that it *had* been thought of, and now that it had started, it was much too fun to stop! With the snowy passageways connecting Room 9's Super Hotel to several others, the mega complex was growing wider than Brewster's Best

Five Star Inn. And with blocks being transported from other hotels in the schoolyard — and with everyone working as one crew — Room 9's Super Hotel would soon be taller than Brewster's, too! The mega crew worked until the last moment of lunch recess. Then they ran right back out to keep on building during the last recess of the day.

As the last recess got underway, Kirby felt his fingers tingle deep within his mitts with excitement. No matter which way you looked at it, near and far, from left to right, up and down and inside, the new snow wonder-structure clearly outshone The Bear's.

But his high spirits soon came crashing down. The Bear, Seth, Darian, and the other denmates had been released for last recess and were now crossing the schoolyard. Instinctively, Kirby, his staff, and the other builders stopped what they were doing and stood up, forming a human wall in front of their work.

The Bear's eyes looked huge as he drank in the sight of the new, never-ending snow hotel.

"*Take . . . it . . . dowwwn!*" The Bear muttered in a low, guttural growl.

"Let's go!" cried Darian, taking two steps forward. "Come on, guys," he snarled, looking around. "Let's *do* this thing!"

"Forget it," mumbled Seth, kicking a patch of snow in front of him. "I'm not giving my recesses up." He walked away from Darian and The Bear, heading for a far corner of the new hotel.

Kirby smiled as Seth approached the mega hotel and inspected one of the new walls. The look on his Grade 6 face even suggested he might be impressed.

One by one, just like Seth, The Bear's minions trickled away. Some headed for The Den, while others blended in with the multi-grade building crew. Kirby watched as The Bear stood in his place a while longer, eyes darting back and forth.

Then, something happened.

Maybe it was the sheer size of the new hotel, or the impossible number of kids he'd have to push through to tear it down. Or maybe The Bear just didn't want to give up recess either. Suddenly, The Bear turned and walked away. He didn't even glance over at his Den as he tramped through the snow. He just passed it and kept walking and walking.

"Whatever," Darian mumbled, trying to look cool and carefree. And failing. He turned and ran after The Bear.

Some kids began to laugh. Some may have even sent the odd taunt in The Bear's direction. Most whooped and cheered and high-fived one another. Then they went straight back to building.

As for Kirby, he dropped into a deep knee bend and clenched his right hand into a fist. He thrust his arm back and forth through the air with exuberance.

"YES!" he shouted so loudly it could have caused an avalanche.

#14
"Think Bigger!"

"NOOO!" Kirby and Marvin cried out in unison. On screen, they were crushed by a boulder for the third time in a row.

"So close!" Marvin groaned, reaching for the open bag of cheese nachos between them. "We've got to beat this level," he said through the crunch of chips. "Let's go again."

"In a minute," Kirby said, putting down his controller. He tapped his finger to his lip and gazed toward his thinking chair where *How to Make Something from Nothing* lay open to the final chapter. He turned back to Marvin. "So, I had this idea . . ."

"Think Bigger!"

Marvin raised his eyebrows.

"You know how awesome the Mega Hotel looks? Almost like a little village or town or something?" Kirby continued. "It got me thinking . . ."

"*O . . . K . . .*" Marvin said very slowly, sounding a little worried.

"Well, what if we made something like that this summer? But not at school — in our front yards."

"In summer? But . . ."

"Not out of snow, of course. Out of — I don't know — big sheets of cardboard and scrap wood and stuff." Kirby rose to his knees as his excitement mounted.

"Sheets of cardboard," Marvin echoed softly with a slight shake of his head.

"We could make a haunted cowboy ghost town — something like that — and charge admission for haunted tours. Or — *oo!*" Kirby was in full chirp-mode now. "We could set up the ghost town in my yard, and sell refreshments to our customers in yours! What do you think?"

"Kirby . . ." Marvin began.

"We'll be rich, Marvin. Rich!" Kirby went on gleefully. "Maybe we should start planning now, and then . . ."

"Or," Marvin interrupted, holding Kirby's controller out to him. "*Maybe* we could finish this level."

Kirby threw another glance at the open book on his chair. As he did, he caught a glimpse of the blustery snow-filled sky beyond his bedroom window. Summer was still many, many months away. Plus, he and Marvin were on a pretty good roll in their game . . .

He tapped his lip and sat back down.

"Good plan," said Kirby. He took his controller from Marvin and pressed *start*. "Let's beat these boulders . . . *big time!*"